Overtime

A Collection of Short Stories

edited by
Jeff Bradley & Marion Goodworth

apprentice
house

Baltimore, Maryland
www.apprenticehouse.com

Apprentice House is an imprint of Resonant Publishing

Edited by Jeff Bradley and Marion Goodworth
Cover design by Michael Barry

First printing
10 9 8 7 6 5 4 3 2 1

ISBN: 1-934074-08-X
13-Digit ISBN: 978-1-934074-08-4

apprentice
house

Baltimore, Maryland
www.apprenticehouse.com

Overtime

A Collection of Short Stories

Contents

Preface • *The Editors*. ix
Foreword • *Ron Tanner* xi
Introduction • *Daniel McGuiness* xiii

Overtime • *Shelly Geatty* 1
Fire Dancing • *Alyssa Milletti* 29
Past Work Experience • *James Palma*. 37
Ordinary Time • *Katie McHugh* 43
The After Dark • *Maryl Roberts*. 61
They should have gone to Tango • *Laurence Ross*. . . . 79
The Spin Cycle • *Aileen DePeter*. 95
Twelve Steps • *Karen Laird* 115
Grown-ups • *Julie Weller* 133
The Small Time • *Laurence Ross* 143
Bagpipes • *Margaret Dougherty* 161

Preface
The Editors

When we started working on this project, we were trying to create an anthology of short fiction that would appeal to a younger audience as well as an adult audience. We decided that the best place to find these stories would be on a college campus because the students are writing stories that are relevant to their lives, while also entertaining an older and more educated audience of faculty. Being students at Loyola College in Maryland, we thought that our own literary magazine – the Garland – would be the best place to look. We read through all of the back issues of the Garland, culling short fiction, poems and photographs. After reading through all the stories we picked what we considered the best and most interesting stories. We think it is important for these stories to be shared with the world because they are full of real life issues and problems and they reflect the thoughts of college aged students, which most people can relate to. Personally I enjoyed all of the stories and think they should be read and enjoyed by a larger audience. The authors deserve recognition for their hard work and hopefully this anthology will give them the credit they deserve.

Marion Goodworth '05

Opportunity is one of the greatest assets available to a college student. Throughout my life I have been privileged to a number of opportunities, everything from a wonderful family to enrollment in an excellent college. Apprentice House publishing is about opportunity on every level. Not only are we providing a forum for aspiring writers, but we attain much-needed experience for ourselves. Experiential learning is the best learning. This book was put through the entire production process; from conceptualization and acquisitions to editing and design, students did it all. I don't know of any other undergraduate program in the country where an opportunity like this is even possible.

With so much focus on opportunity, it seemed appropriate to provide one for Loyola student writers. Long has our college had a strong writing program, and we wanted to show off a little with a collection of writing from our annual literary journal. The stories within this book were chosen because they were strong, and we felt they went a long way in representing good Loyola fiction.

I would like to thank personally all of our contributors, who bore with us over the months as we approached our deadline and encountered all the things that publishers encounter. And for you, good readers, I hope you will find enjoyment in these craft-full stories.

Here's to opportunity.

Jeff Bradley '05

Foreword

Ron Tanner

We who teach writing at Loyola College know one thing above all others: Loyola students write very well. In fact, they write well when they come to us in their first year. Happily, they write even better when they leave us in their fourth. Reading this collection of stories from ten years' worth of the Garland, the Writing Department's literary magazine of fiction and poetry, I am proud to be associated with these students and proud especially to have helped several of them with their story drafts.

On behalf of the Writing faculty, I would <u>like</u> to claim credit for their successes. But I really can't make this claim. We teachers must admit that, while we may be able to teach students how to use certain techniques and strategies, we cannot teach talent. What you will find in these stories, then, is not only the product of study and practice—what we strive to take from class—but also the expression of talent. The credit for this belongs to the writers alone.

Thematically, these stories range widely, from adultery to first love, from the humorous to the nearly-tragic, and they include central characters of an equally wide spectrum: a child, a teenager, a college student, a nurse, an electrician, a legal secretary, among others. One of the many strengths I see in these stories is the use of local, familiar landmarks and places. No stories take place in Tibet or Somalia, for instance, because these writers know that exotic locations can distract a writer, not to mention a reader, from the important stuff—what happens to the people in the story. It is likewise with exotic occupations. Hence, you will find no sorcerers or international spies in these stories. On the contrary, you will find more than one story that takes place in Maryland and more than one story that deals with the day-to-day travails of working life. These are the most difficult stories to write precisely because their terrain is so ordinary. Which is to say that these writers have set for themselves the largest challenges.

The greatest of these challenges is to plumb the depths of character and examine the workings of the human heart and mind at the point of conflict. In doing this, these writers offer us a glimpse of ourselves through the lives of others. That's the appeal of a truly good story: we care about the characters, we root for their success, and we feel for them when, inevitably, all does not go as planned or hoped for. This is not to say that the short story tradition that our Loyola writers sustain is gloomy or fatalistic; it is to say, rather, that these writers engage life fully, embracing its complexities. What makes these stories enjoyable, in other words, is the same thing that makes life enjoyable: their complexities yield surprises and the surprises, even when they stop us short, gratify us ultimately because it is only then--at the confluence of pain and confusion, love and longing—that we know we are most alive.

May you enjoy the good work of our Loyola writers in this collection and discover yet more to admire as you return to their stories in the years to come.

Ron Tanner, Chair
Writing Department
April 10, 2005

Introduction

Daniel McGuiness

Fiction

>The people in the elevator all
>Face front, they all keep still, they all
>Look up with the rapt and stupid look of saints
>In paintings at the numbers that light up
>By turn and turn to tell them where they are.
>They are doing the dance, they are playing the game.
>
>To get here they have gone by avenue
>And street, by ordinate and abscissa, and now
>By this new coordinate, up. They are three-
>Dimensional characters, taken from real life;
>They have their fates, whether to rise or fall,
>And when their numbers come up they get out.

Howard Nemerov (1975)

Remember the Nineteenth Century?
Now THAT was a century!
Internal Combustion.
Imperialism
The Bustle
The Novel

Remember the Novel?

Austen-esque novels
Dickension novels
Hardy (party) novels
Now that was a genre!

"The hidden life is, by definition, hidden. The hidden life that appears in external signs is hidden no longer, has entered the realm of action. And it is the function of the novelist to reveal the hidden life at its source: to tell us more about Queen Victoria than could be known, and thus to produce a character who is not the Queen Victoria of history"

> *E. M. Forster*
> Aspects of the Novel (1927)

We haven't got the times for a long sitdown and a hefty tome. We haven't got the Nineteenth Century for crying out loud. The photographers stole the landscape from the painters and the novelists stole the epic from the poets. What's left? Watercolors? Shortstories? The woods are burning, boys.

What you hold in your hands is fiction: pieces of untruth spun together into allusion. Bits and pieces. Spinning. In the Nineteenth Century that was a good word. Homespun. In the Twentieth Century? Not so much. It's a new way to lie, a trap without a spider. Kurds and weigh.

What you hold in your hands is made by writers who happen to be students. At Loyola College in Maryland. I am the introduction. I'll just need another moment of your times:

From "Dead Souls"

> When figures from the past stand tall
> And mocking voices ring the hall
> Imperialistic house of prayer
> Conquistadors who took their share
>
> They keep calling me
> Keep on calling me
> They keep calling me
> Keep calling me

Nineteenth Century. . .
    Nineteenth. . .
        Nine. . .
            Nin. . .
                NIN

Reznor rules.

Overtime

Shelly Geatty

It was a week-long story that happened one night and should have ended with my life, but didn't. Everyone at the shop still talks about what happened and they really rag on Rick because he just hauled ass and left me on the roof with four convicted criminals. Damn right I left, Rick says, someone would have to be alive to identify the body.

"It had been one hell of a week between leaving at four in the morning to work on a busted front-end loader in Fredericksburg and running all the way back to Glen Burnie by noon to try and put the crane back together that was supposed to be done last week. I couldn't sleep for figuring how it'd all get done, not that I had much time to sleep anyway. By Friday, I was so tired I couldn't find my ass with both hands and by six o'clock that night the last thing I wanted to hear was that something else was busted. I had just walked into the office to tell Al that I was packing up for the day when he tells me he'd gotten an emergency call from the prison warden who's panicked because the routine service check showed that one of their generators was down. Rick and I were the last ones dumb enough to still be around the shop past quitting time and sure enough, the next thing we knew, we had loaded up the truck, cranked up the AC and headed down 95, nursing two jumbo 7-11 coffees and fighting rush hour traffic.

My luck, I thought, Friday night at a maximum security prison. There was a Bud Light with my name on it at the bar across the river and I could almost taste it, but tonight was looking like all I'd be drinking was coffee, black, and lots of it. I could understand why the warden wanted us down there, though, because if the prison goes dark with no generator, I sure as hell wouldn't want to be there. The clouds were looking a little too dark for comfort and in mid-July you never know when a storm could turn into one of those unreasonable hurricane-type things that are usually named after women. Of course, only a government institution would pick a Friday afternoon to check their generators, so just in case one's broken there'd be nobody around to do repairs. I was working up to a real bad mood, and knew Rick was going to start about our prospects for the evening, and he didn't disappoint me. He lit a Marlboro Light and squinted at me.

"You know, this is the second week in a row Al's pulled this on me." He shook his head and flicked an ash out the window. "I'm in for a reamin' when I get home." He was probably right, I knew from experience. There was nothing like being caught between your job and your wife - either way you went one of them was going to dump you.

"You call her yet?"

"Na, haven't worked up the nerve."

I didn't blame him for not wanting to face Donna. Things wouldn't have been so bad if he didn't work days while she worked nights. This was the second Friday night she had gotten somebody to stand in for her, only to get stood up again and Rick could bet even money he was sleeping on the couch that night. He took another drag of the cigarette and I rolled down my window to get some air. I was trying to quit, trying real hard. My daughter Audrey, in all her eight years, had never seen me drink a beer or smoke a cigarette but Heather had gone and told her that I smoked, so I promised I'd quit. I'd do anything for that girl, and even if she didn't know it, this was one of the most difficult ways I'd ever try to prove it.

"Hey," Rick said, noticing that I was daydreaming and giving me a sideways glance, "you taking Ginny to the company picnic? She's dying for you to ask her."

Oh no, I thought, dangerous ground. There are three things I don't like talking about - Unions, politics, and women. Personally, I'd given up on women, and some of them had already returned the favor. "No," I said, as disinterested as possible, "she's not my type."

I Rick snorted and rolled his eyes at me. "What is your type?"

I figured he wasn't going to give this up, so the only I way around a sore subject was my usual asshole attitude. "A nymphomaniac who owns a liquor store."

Rick shook his head and took another drag of his cigarette. "Why don't you just take her to the picnic? It's not like getting married again or anything. Just get out some, get away from the goddamn shop."

"Yeah," I said, checking my rearviews to switch lanes, "Get away from the shop to go to a company picnic with the boss's secretary. What a treat."

"Beats spending the day with a transmission."

"Not really, at least you can make some sense out of a tranny."

He flicked the remains of the cigarette out the window and scowled at me. "Not every woman is out to screw you over, you know."

"I said I would think about it."

My best plan was changing the subject or turning up the radio. Rick meant well, but I didn't need more hassle in my life, and I certainly didn't need another woman complicating things, especially one I worked with. It had only been a year since the separation, and dating seemed too much like being unfaithful. During the week, when I wasn't working for L&S, I'd take side jobs so I didn't have to go home and have time to think about things like women or lawyer bills. The guys I shared the apartment with hardly ever saw me during the week, because I usually got home around nine or ten and left again at five or six. The only time I didn't work was Saturdays when I picked up Audrey. Heather leaving really had made me realize just how important my time was with my daughter, and I guess if anything good came out of this whole separation thing, I'm really putting everything into being a good dad.

Traffic through the tunnel wasn't moving and Rick and I were both pricked out about taking half an hour to get somewhere fifteen minutes away. Al, exercising his usual patience, had already called on the truck phone to ask why the hell we weren't there yet. They were getting white knuckles at the prison, and security had called the shop to make sure we were double timing. Much as we were in a hurry, when we pulled up at the main gate we stopped for a minute just to take it all in. Absolutely creepy. The prison sprawled across seven or eight acres, surrounded by two ten foot fences coiled with razor wire. Several low brick buildings butted against each other and in the cells you could make out the prisoners moving back and forth behind the bars. A few guards stood sentry in the gun towers, and about a dozen or more were standing around the main entrance. Another paced between the fences with a German Shepherd. Nothing about the place was particularly inviting, and the way the sky was looking meaner didn't help matters any.

"Shit," Rick drawled, giving the gun tower a sideways glance, "Nobody's getting out of here fast."

I laughed because I figured Rick didn't quite know

where we were. This wasn't jail, this was prison and there's a big difference. "Nobody's getting out of here ever, man. This place is maximum security - Lifers."

"Beat," he observed, squinting at a sign posted near the gate, "Caution, drug sniffing dogs patrolling the premises. I tell you what, no dog's sniffin' me. I hate dogs. They can just take my word for it." He eyed the Shepherd again, this time looking a little more anxiously. Rick was pretty short and a little round, so the way he kind of shrunk down in the seat reminded me of the Pillsbury Doughboy with a beard.

"They won't take your word on anything," I said, trying not to laugh, cause I knew he really was afraid of dogs, "They count the number of screwdrivers we have in this truck and we better come out with fifteen if we went in with fifteen, or the whole place is locked down . I tight till they find it."

I guess if I weren't so tired I'd of been a little more upset about being at the prison, at night, with a storm coming in, but the only thing really concerning me was where I was going to fill my tanker sized coffee cup before I passed out. Right then I was about twenty hours short on sleep for the week, so I tried to keep awake by watching the entrance exam for the prison. In front of us was a laundry truck being searched while the driver was emptying out his pockets inside the security booth. One guard was walking the edge of the truck with a mirror suspended on a long pole, scanning the undercarriage for weapons, drugs or unwanted passengers, while a second guard was itemizing the contents of the cab and checking his count against the list on his clipboard. I knew exactly what we were in for, so I figured maybe I could take a nap while they counted the eleven hundred odd tools I had rolling around in the bins of my service truck.

"Man, they take this shit serious," Rick said, digging

into the pound bag of M&M's he kept as a co-pilot I on the road, and watching the driver replace his wallet and leave the security booth.

"Well, after last month I guess so. A prisoner got killed in a fight down here with a t-wrench some contractor left. They knew it was missing, searched every cell but they didn't find it till some guy planted it in another guy's lung." Truth, too, but I figured I should quit while Rick was still with me. He was starting to crack his knuckles, a sure sign he was getting nervous, and a sure way to irritate the hell out of me. I took the last swig of my coffee, dying for a cigarette and hoping the caffeine would kick in soon. The guard was waving us into what they affectionately called the cage just as the laundry truck pulled past us. The driver leaned out his window, eyed up my truck and laughed, "Good luck, pal."

"Thanks man," I said, pulling past the gate and rolling down the window for the guard who came over with his clipboard. The cage was about fifteen feet high, completely enclosed - top, too - with a chain link fence. On our left was the guard station, a long, low brick building with bullet proof glass looking out into the cage. . Most of the guards were sitting around, patronizing the snack machines, and looking generally useless. On our other side was nothing but concrete, but if you look up you got a great view of the three guys in the gun tower with their shot guns trained on you. Before the guard could speak the gate slammed shut behind us and Rick and I both just about jumped out of our skins because it sounded like a basketball slammed against the chain link fence right next to our heads.

"Evenin' sir, state your name and business please," the guard mumbled, obviously having built up a tolerance to the noise of the cage. His gut was pushing against the buttons on his uniform, and I was thinking I hope he doesn't have to apprehend any quick-moving criminals, because he wouldn't have a Honda's chance 1 at a Harley convention of catching any. "Jeff," I said,

"L&S Diesel. We're here to fix the generator. Supposed to meet the electrical engineer and the Warden."

"Oh, you guys. What took you so damn long? Warden's been checking in every five minutes looking for you."

That's gratitude for you - Friday night, stuck in traffic, not even on call, and I get this raft of shit from a police academy reject. My patience was wearing thin. "Well, Sir, it's rush hour on a Friday. Traffic was backed from here to the hinges of Hell. We got here fast as we could."

"Hold on a minute here, son." He fiddled with his radio, got the warden and told him we were here. Son. Damn, that pissed me off. Thirty-four, a beard, a few

crow's feet I'm right proud of and he calls me son. You got to love what a badge can do for a man, or to him, in this case.

"Listen here, boy," he said, looking around for anybody waiting outside the cage, "this did not happen. Warden says he needed you a half hour ago. You got any drugs, explosives, or weapons on your person?"

Boy... this guy was definitely pushing his luck. "No sir, nothing on my person," I answered, gritting my teeth while Rick nodded in his agreement.

"All right, get your ass in there. There's an Administrative Building to your left. Courtyard, E Wing. Can't miss it. Lee and the Warden are waiting in the office." He pointed past the first gun tower. "Straight through he gate and a hard left. Hope you work right fast, son." He glanced at the gathering clouds and hitched his pants around what used to be his waist.

"Fast as we can without getting fried... son." Okay, can be an asshole when I want to, and I'm pretty good at it, but this guy was asking for it. I tipped my L&S hat ! ;0 him and tried real hard to wipe the smirk off my face. As we pulled out of the cage and through the main entrance, the gate slammed shut behind us and there was no doubt we were on the inside looking out.

"That was what they call maximum security?" Rick asked, looking back toward the guards milling around the cage. "I thought we were going to get the third degree."

"No, that was maximum security scared shitless that their backup generator isn't going to be able to back them up," I said, thinking of a hundred and one interesting ways to get killed by a sufficiently armed convict. "They must want us in here real bad, 'cause you know that should have never happened."

"I heard that," Rick grumbled, looking around like this was the last place he wanted to be right then. This wasn't exactly my first choice for Friday night either, but the responsibilities that came with this job didn't always fit into 9 to 5. Of course, wives didn't always understand that, and most of the guys at the shop had found out the hard way, including me. I needed the challenge I got here, though, guess now I was almost addicted to it. Always under the gun, either on a Coast Guard ship, an Amtrak train, or a quarry crane, there was a rush that went with the emergencies we got thrown into.

When we pulled up Lee, the electrical engineer, was busy pacing around outside the Administrative building. "'Bout time, you sorry excuse for an emergency service. What the hell did you do, stop for a little dinner and dancing on the way down here?"

I couldn't decide if he was looking angry or scared. "Well Lee, what's it been, about two weeks since we worked on the last piece of shit you guys busted? I figured you wouldn't want to see me so soon."

"Yeah, well, this is not a clogged fuel filter. This generator is dead." Lee was a tall guy, black hair with a lot of gray creeping in, and he looked a lot like Ward Cleaver in overalls. When he got fired up he turned bright red and all I could do was laugh, which didn't help matters any. But Lee wasn't my main concern. The warden, a real big irate looking black guy in a suit and tie, was stomping down the stairs and taking up more of my attention.

"If you two are through with the cordialities, maybe we can take a look at this generator. I got a prison to run here, you know." He had a permanent scowl and looked about two years overdue for a vacation. Definitely not someone you want to tangle with, so, of course, I couldn't resist. I mean, he didn't have to get in my face when I was here to help him.

"From what I heard, you're going to be running a convict roundup if we don't get you some backup power. I thought you'd be real glad to see us."

"Real glad," he growled, "But your goddamn Union, foul mouthed attitude I can do without."

"If I were Union, I'd be busy holding down a bar stool and you'd be sweating it out alone... Sir."

I knew I was getting in too deep, but I had never been known for thinking before speaking. This guy was pissing me off. But, I figured this was a bad time to be making enemies, so I tried to smooth things over a little. "Regardless, I'm here to help you out. Lee and I were just reminiscing."

The warden put a little more effort into his scowl. "You're lucky I'm too busy to get into it right now, pal." Loosening his tie, he stalked off, not stopping to check if we were following him. I was counting off the reasons why I shouldn't just slug him, when Rick shot me a look like - don't even think about it. I took a deep breath and we followed Lee and the warden into E-Wing. Just before the main entrance we stopped and rang the bell to the gate, and waited while Barney Fife's twin took out this big old skeleton key about the size of my fist to let us in. Through the gate, we walked up to a door that looked a lot like it should be on the front of the Adams Family's house. All I could think was - if Lurch answers the door I'm out of here, job or no job. We went down a long corridor and out into the courtyard. Once we were outside, the big steel double doors slammed shut behind us and we were completely enclosed by E-Wing's four corridors. All around us barred windows looked out onto this ten by ten patch of grass with nothing but a big gray hunk of steel for landscaping. It took me about ten minutes to look into the jungle of wires and the main engine to diagnose the problem. Twelve years on every kind of engine you can think of had made me pretty fast and pretty damn good at what I did, and as I saw the hole in the side of the engine block, I knew this was going to be one hell of a night.

"You're right, Lee. DOA - dead on her ass. You know, maybe you should put your maintenance people in charge of executions. They're so damned efficient." I was getting tired of coming in here to clean up after the incompetent bastards that were home with their families not giving a damn about what happened once they punched out while I was stuck here - on salary, mind you, we don't get overtime pay - trying to fix some catastrophe basic maintenance procedures could have prevented. I was hot, and I really didn't mean to take the whole thing out on Lee, so I took a deep breath and switched to my most professional demeanor.

"Crankshaft's busted," I said, shaking my head over the tangle of fried wires I had pulled out to get to the engine, "There is not a thing you can do. Money'd be better spent to get a whole new generator then to replace the engine in this dinosaur." I hated to break it to them, and I hated even worse that I couldn't fix the thing, mostly because this was going to be an all-nighter getting a rental in here to back them up. Audrey had a 9 o'clock soccer game tomorrow morning, and it was looking like I wasn't going to be there.

"Nothing?" the warden asked, looking at me like I was the dumb son of a bitch who had broken the thing.

"Nada. What's this hooked up to?" I figured since they had three or four generators, there was a shot that maybe this one was wired to the cafeteria or the laundry room or something insignificant like that, maybe the warden's personal entertainment center.

"The entire E- Wing. Both corridors. The main lock down. Any more questions?"

"None except how fast can you get a P.O.?" This was getting serious. Rick looked at me like - this can't get any worse, right? I looked back at him just as I felt the first couple of drops of rain and thought, somebody tell me that's a bird going over. The warden glanced up at the gray and black clouds cruising in from the West and bearing down pretty fast, then he looked back at me.

"Got the scenario now? We got a bad storm coming through here. Get your guys on the job and don't worry about the Purchase Order. I'll have one by the time you bring the rental in here."

I studied him real hard, weighing his situation against mine. If I brought a rental in here with no P.O. and the warden's bureaucratic tap dance didn't work, the bill was coming out of my paycheck - if I still had a job. "I can't do that and you know it," I said, "We've been screwed on this before. No P.O. no go. I'm sorry, I can't." I didn't want to let him down but I wasn't putting my ass on a 7,000 dollar line. No way, for nobody. I was going to put Audrey through the best college in the country so that she wouldn't have to put up with this kind of crap, and I wasn't risking my paycheck for any reason. Thunder growled off in the distance and the sky was getting dark so they threw the flood lights on in the courtyard. The warden's radio spat and crackled out something about a disturbance in the building to our right, and he swore a blue streak I had to admire. He ran his hand through the remainder of his hair and squeezed his eyes tight.

"Look, I'll get the money if I have to pay for it myself," he grumbled. There was something in his voice, maybe in the way he looked about ten years older than when we had walked in, that much as I didn't like the guy, I believed he wouldn't screw me on this one. Still, this was a field decision and either way I went, I was probably going to lose. Al would fire me if I went ahead without a P.O., but then again he'd fire me if I didn't get them a backup. I glanced up at the clouds that looked about ready to break, then over at the shadows of prisoners pacing back and forth behind the bars like animals in a zoo.

"God bless it," I sighed, shaking my head, "All right, but I'm really taking a chance here. We got to get you wired to the rental. Seems your government engineers built this building around the generator, so that just in case it goes down, you'll need the mother of all cranes to get it out. We don't have that kind of time for that and I'd have to guess you don't want me running cable through the main doors and leaving 'em open for a day or two. The only other way to go is up." I squinted through the drizzle at the top of E- Wing. "Can you get me up on that roof?"

"Whatever you have to do. I can get you clearance. I can get you anything you need." Anything I need? How about a life, I thought, can he get me one of those? The warden shot a look at Lee, who was chewing on his lip and contemplating the guts of the generator. "Lee, don't let smart ass and his buddy here out of your sight."

The three of us watched the Warden stomp off to

tend to his disturbance and kiss ass for a P.O. "Who pissed in his Wheaties this morning?" I asked Lee, hoping to lighten things up a little. Somebody had to. Lee sighed and shook his head. "That's just his usual congenial self. What part of the roof do you want?"

"No part," Rick piped up, looking like he was shocked I had even considered the idea, "I don't do roofs."

"You do now," I said, giving him a friendly push toward the building.

"Hold up, now." Lee was jogging to keep up with us. "We can't just go strolling around on the top of building here. I got to get clearance."

"Well, do your thing," I said, not slowing up. When there was a job to do, I wanted to get it done and I figured Lee could walk and talk at the same time. We made our way through the corridors of the E-Wing while Lee got on his radio. "Gun Tower one, report please." The radio hissed and spat before the voice came over.

"Gun Tower one, reporting."

"I've got two contractors and a supervisor on E-Wing roof, east side. Repeat, please."

"Gun Tower one - two contractors and a supervisor on E-Wing roof, east side, confirmed."

"Gun Tower two, repeat and confirm please."

"Gun Tower two - two contractors and a supervisor on E- Wing roof, east side, confirmed."

Lee was still calling into the towers when Rick, who had been busy peering past the main corridor and down the halls that were made up of long lines of cells, started paying attention to the security process. "Talk about your formalities. Can't he just call to all of them once?"

"Sure, he could. One of them could hear wrong, too. If the gun towers don't think we should be up there they're going to shoot first and worry about who it was later."

Rick's eyes got about the size of the hubcaps on my

truck. "You sure they all heard right?"

"Not my job. Ask Lee." We got to the end of the east corridor of E-Wing and climbed up the steel staircase to the roof. By the time we got up there I was convinced I needed a new job. From where we stood, we had a bird's eye view of the dead hunk of steel in the middle of the courtyard, about a hundred feet from the roof, and it was pretty clear there was absolutely no other way to wire them back up than to pull cable from the other side of the building up over the roof. That was if we could get the flatbed towing the rental generator onto the prison grounds. Right behind E-Wing and directly below us was an old maintenance gate that looked big enough to fit the truck through, but it was also two days older than God, had a coating of vines about a foot deep, and was planted smack in the middle of a mud farm because of all the rain we'd been having. But, that was our only shot at getting a working generator in close enough, so it was a plan. After we climbed down off the roof, Lee wandered off to break the news to the Warden, and Rick and I walked over to my truck to call in the flatbed driver. Halfway across the parking lot, Rick just cracked.

"You aren't serious, right? I mean, you're whacked if you think we're going to pull half a ton of cable over I that roof. That's two stories. Count 'em, two!" He pointed toward the roof, evidently waiting for the height of the building to hit me, then I'd suddenly change my mind, go home, prop my feet up and watch reruns of MASH. "Not to mention a hundred feet across the roof I and another hundred across the yard," he continued, his first attempt to shake me was failing, "That's if we can even get those gates open. Last time those things were used, Colonel Sanders was a Lieutenant. You're a fry short of a happy meal, man, you've lost it." Rick was rambling, the way he always did when he got all worked up. When he finally realized I wasn't changing my mind he shut up, stuffed his hands in his pockets and shook his head.

"You've always known I needed a check up from the neck up," I took my hat, pulled my comb from my back pocket, ran it through my hair which was steadily working past my shoulders. "All I know is, we got to get this done."

Rick stopped walking and gawked at me. "On our time, all we have to do is pay taxes and die. Personally I'd rather not do either of them tonight. I'm not on call and by my watch, this is my time. Tell the Warden we'll have a crew by morning."

"Haven't you figured it out by now? Al's time is Monday through Monday." I wasn't going to let Rick cut out on me now, and I had to let him know how it was. "Look, we're here. I'm not taking the chance on this place going down. We got a storm coming though and if I can't get a crew, I'll pull the damn cable myself."

"Jeff, you need a reality check. You need to chill. You're asking me to make like a lightning rod on a roof or be a pin cushion for some pissed off convict whose lawyer may have looked kind of like you. You're just plain asking for it, man." He looked at me from under the brim of his crumpled L&S Diesel hat, scrunching up his face and trying to figure me. Finally he came up with his verdict. "You are not normal."

"I never claimed to be normal." I was starting to feel the past couple of days catching up to me then, and I wasn't in the mood to argue. "Look, this job is just about all I have left in life, and I'm not going to screw it up. Just relax and eat your M&M's."

We got in the truck and I paged PC from the truck phone, because he, much like me, didn't have a life and I knew he was the only one in my crew who would call back on a Friday night. Good old Pork Chop, he'd always call back unless you caught him at dinner. After I made sure PC could get the 2500 pounds of cable up on the flatbed with the fork lift, I pulled my hat down over my - eyes and tried to get some sleep. I wasn't going to get into it with Rick right then. When I get tired, my defenses start breaking down. I mean, how do you defend something you love but you downright hate, that eats away at you like this goddamn job. I couldn't work on cars in some hick town gas station. The engines I worked on were generally bigger than cars, and I got called in for emergency jobs four or five states away because I knew my shit. In fact, I had just gotten another job offer from a trucking company I did moonlighting for. Better pay, less hours, even overtime pay. Trouble was, I'd just be doing engine work, nothing like the emergency calls I was used to. I know what Heather would say, that I didn't know when to call it quits. Maybe she was right, but I just didn't want to take a chance on another job. At that point, L&S was about the only thing that was really stable in my life.

I woke up from my nap ten minutes later when Lee I and the warden came over to tell us they had gotten the go-ahead for our plan. The warden was starting to look a little less stressed, at least the vein in his temple wasn't pumping anymore. I figured this was a good time to tell him we were never going to get the generator wired without some more man power, since we had about 2500 pounds of cable to pull.

"Manpower?" He tilted his head toward the cell blocks: "We got men here with nothing but time. I'm sure I can convince them that they'd be glad to help you. What'd you need?" Loaded question. A life, a vacation, a raise, definitely a cigarette but I decided to keep my professional demeanor with this guy, who was far from my biggest fan. "I already have one guy coming in to off load the flatbed. I need another to help with that, four more to hump it up on the roof."

"Not a problem. I'll have some guys sent out to you."

Walking off toward the administration building, he left Lee, Rick and me to wait it out in the drizzle that was just starting working up to a decent rain. I told Rick to start getting PC checked in at the cage to save us some time. He grumbled something about not having eaten supper yet so Lee took him over to security with the promise of going to the cafeteria afterwards. Meanwhile, I was about ready to pass out. I stretched out in the front seat and was just about unconscious when I heard the rain start pelting the roof of the truck which wasn't so bad because the rain would wash the sweat off. It was the thunder that worried me, though, because a roof is not the best place to be in a lightning storm.

I sat up to see how the sky was looking just as the double doors swung open. Light flooded the parking lot, then it took me a minute to make out what all of a sudden blocked the doorway. It was actually a man shouldering through the door jams, and my next thought was, Good God, what did they convict Paul Bunyan for? This guy was huge, I mean, if you want to talk about the genetic pool, he was definitely swimming in the deep end. His bicep was about the size of my head, and when he walked out of the building I had to wonder why he didn't just pick up his guard and toss him into the next county. The guard left his charge standing under the awning and walked over to me.

"I take it you're the contractor who needs help?"

"Yes sir," I said pushing up the brim of my hat, "I definitely need help."

"Good, I got four more coming down in a little while."

"Thank you, kindly." The guard went back to get the rest of his crew and I sat there just staring at the prisoner he had left behind. Funny how they'd take a half hour to search a laundry truck, but they leave a prisoner standing not three feet from me. Then again, the only guns were up in the gun towers, so the guards were useless as sliding glass doors on a submarine. No wonder they couldn't get good help around here. My truck wasn't three feet from the awning, so the prisoner nodded and stepped toward me. "Guard said I'm supposed to be helping you. What'd you have in mind?"

"Well, got some cable to pull up over that roof there." Squinting up at the roof he said, "No problem." He nodded and stepped back, like it wasn't his place to be talking to me. Somehow, I didn't think the cable would be a problem for him. The guy could probably toss me and my truck up on the roof, but he didn't seem like the type to throw his weight around. He was just standing there with his arms crossed in front of his chest -which was about three feet across - getting rained on; his t-shirt looked like it could double for a car cover. He didn't make another move, didn't say another word. Now me, I've always been the talkative type. We'd been on a lot of jobs where they bring in grunt labor to help us. I would always bullshit with them, just to be friendly. I figured, what could happen? At least with someone to talk to I'd stay awake.

"Why don't you go ahead and pull some truck up under you, pal? Tad bit drier in here."

He looked at me for a second, like he wasn't sure why I was asking. Finally he said, "Don't mind if I do." He came around to the other side and when he passed in front of the headlights and all I could think was hope the truck holds up under his weight. He was nothing but solid muscle. When he got in I could see his face pretty well. He couldn't have been over twenty-five or twenty-six, real good looking kid, sandy blonde, clean cut, clean shaven.

"Thanks a lot, man." He put out his hand, which was as calloused as mine. I chalked that up to the lifting he must be doing.

"No problem. I'm Jeff." His grip turned out to be strong but not the crunch I had expected.

"Mark. Good to meet you."

"Same." And I really was glad to have someone to talk to besides Rick and the warden. Both of them were starting to wear on the one nerve I had left. There wasn't much that leaped right out as conversation, so I started with the obvious. "You ever pull cable?"

He shook his head, occasionally glancing toward the double doors where he had been standing. "Laid some underground cable. Don't know if that's the same or not. I worked for a contractor up in Columbia for almost a year."

"Right church, wrong pew. This cable's just as heavy, though. Who'd you work for in Columbia?"

"Henkles and McCoy. We did a lot of office buildings." He cocked his head to the side and knotted up his brow like an old man trying to remember the details of a story from a long time ago. Town was starting to build up and we had more work than we knew what to do with. In fact, we put bids on that Marley Station place they were going to build in Glen Bumie. Did they ever finish that?"

"Finish it?" He floored me with that one. Marley Station had been one of the biggest malls in Maryland for over six years now and he was talking about just putting in bids? This guy had been on the inside for a while. "Yeah, it's pretty well finished." I paused, groping for something to say. "Real big place, beautiful too. You ought to go see it when you get outta here."

Mark's voice dropped a couple octaves deeper and he didn't look right at me when he said, "I'm not getting out of here." His hands were resting on his knees and he was looking down at the black prison issue shoes that had to be a size thirteen. I was just then aware that this wasn't some guy they sent down from maintenance to work with us on a job. He was in here for a reason. What was I thinking? For Christ sake, I was the one who had told Rick when we pulled in - Lifers - nobody you'd want to meet in a dark alley, probably nobody you'd want to sit in a truck with. But there was nothing about Mark that if I met him on the outside I'd peg him for a criminal. He was super polite, nice to meet you, and all. It was like, to make up for all that muscle, he made a point of being quiet, standing with his arms crossed, staying in the shadows like he didn't really want to be noticed or singled out. Meanwhile, I had just managed to make a royal ass of myself. I forgot, I just flat out forgot.

"I'm sorry, man. I really didn't mean to say anything that would…"

"Hey, don't sweat it." He looked up at me and smiled like he was glad we had gotten the obvious out and done with. "If you go trying to think about every thing you say like that we'll never get anything said." The cars passing on the road outside the prison caught his attention and he was quiet for a minute. Finally he said, "You know, I've been in here for eight years, and it's like the world just freezes like you remember it. You forget everything's all going on out there." He turned to look at me, and I could only see half his face because of the shadows. "I used to hunt in those woods with my j dad, every Thanksgiving, right there where they wanted to clear for the mall."

I made sure I kept up his gaze. "No woods there anymore. Whole area is pretty built up now. Columbia too, nothing but office buildings and yuppie complexes."

"Figures. We used to bow hunt back there. Beautiful land."

Eying up the size of his biceps, I couldn't resist saying something. "I bet you don't have any problems drawing back a compound bow." He laughed and looked down at his arm that was bulging against the seams of his t-shirt. "Well, I can lift a pound or two. But there isn't much to do around here but lift. Works out the frustration."

The doors creaked open in front of us and four more guys walked out with the guard. Three of them didn't look much older than Mark, but by their permanent scowls and the three inch scar across the one guy's face they looked downright nasty. They were lean, but built up like they lifted, and one guy curled up his lip in almost a snarl when he asked the guard, "What the hell we doing here?" The last prisoner looked to be about 40, rode hard and put up wet. Standing a little away from the other three, his mouth was pressed into a thin line, his hands at his sides rolling into fists, flattening, then rolling back into fists. He fit more the role of a hardened criminal than Mark did, more like a guy I wouldn't trust as far as I could throw. Not that I could have thrown Mark very far, or even picked him up for that matter, but I pretty much liked him. What I didn't like was the thunder rolling around sounding like it was just getting warmed up.

Mark looked up at the other prisoners. "That's the rest of the crew. I better get over there."

"No, stay here where it's dry. Rentalk won't be here for a couple more minutes yet, and there's no use getting a head start on getting rained on. Greaseman show's coming on in a few minutes."

"Greaseman? I used to listen to him every night. I thought they'd have kicked him off the air waves by now."

He shot another glance toward the guard, who didn't seem too worried by the absence of a prisoner. Odds were, he hadn't even noticed. .. Jeff, I'd like to stay, man, but it's probably not a good idea to be in here. I better go stand with the other guys where the guard can keep an eye on me."

"Well, I guess I'll see you enough up on the roof."

"Yeah, man. Thanks for the sit down."

We shook hands again before he left. As Mark walked over to join his crew, I could see PC coming through the cage with the flatbed full of cable and towing the rental so I figured I'd better get myself in gear and do something useful. When he drove up, I filled him f' in on the grand scheme to get this place wired up and I thanked him for the foot long barker and jumbo coffee he had brought me from 7-11. Pork Chop knew me and he knew I wouldn't have gotten around to eating yet. Not that a chili dog was going to do anything but kick up my ulcer, but I guess I wasn't quite through making myself suffer yet. We were crowding time, so when Lee and Rick came back we rounded up the prisoners and started to get set up for work. Lee called in a guard to escort us to the roof, and this guy looked too much like Rosco P. Coltrain from the Dukes of Hazard, but with a bigger beer gut and about ten years past his retirement. The guard went through the whole fun tower routine again, this time with two contractors, one guard, and four prisoners, repeat and confirm towers one through four.

After a few tries and some assurances from me that he couldn't drive a hot nail through a snow bank, PC finally managed to fit the flatbed, generator in tow, through the rusted old maintenance gate and backed up to the building. PC and the remaining prisoner started by knotting a rope around one end of the cable and throwing the other end up to us while a guard sat there and watched them work. On the roof, we teamed up, two at a time pulling while the others rested. After about two hours of hauling hundred and fifty, two hundred pounds of cable at a time straight up onto the roof, we were all ready to fall over soaking wet, and still sweating to death because the July heat wasn't going to let up just for a thunderstorm. I had some quality pain working in the knee I had busted up last year - busted three times because I kept going back to work before it had healed, but who's really counting- and I was close to admitting that I might be dragging a little. We had a couple of good lightning strikes off to the east and the best part of the storm looked like it was yet to come. With all the work, Mark and I didn't have time to talk much, but I was glad he was on my team. The guy didn't quit, and he pulled like an elephant, unlike the other three 'volunteers,' who grumbled and complained the whole time. They weren't exactly the kind of guys you wanted to piss off too bad, so we kept our mouths shut and put up with them. The other thing holding us up was PC and his damned knots on the end of the cable that we couldn't f get untied. Of course, he wasn't real patient with us either.

"What the hell are you doing up there? I want to get home before tomorrow, you know!" He was shouting up at me from the flatbed, looking ridiculous in the rain gear we had all put on because we finally got sick of being drenched.

"Don't count on it…and if you would quit tying your damn girl scout knots maybe I could get the rope back down to you," I shouted through the rain, wrestling with another impossible knot.

"Well, pulling a rope straight up from a roof in the rain will tend to tighten a knot. Deal with it."

"Thanks a heap, asshole." I could always count on Pork Chop for support. I threw back the hood that was blocking my light and laid into the knot again while the rain flattened my hair down into my eyes. By then, I was cursing that granny-knot and its whole knot family. I was crowding thirty hours without sleep and didn't have much left to give. My vote was for the most efficient way to get something done and get some sleep. I yanked at the rope a few more times, then got down on one knee - the one that was left - and started giving it hell. The rain was beatin' on us pretty good, not a downpour but enough to soak you through. The lightning kept getting closer, and I couldn't get a decent grip on the rope, so I took the next logical step. Without even thinking what I was doing, I reached under my rain gear, unsnapped my Buck knife and flipped out the blade. The second the blade clicked, everyone just froze. Even in the rain, everybody on that roof could hear the sound of a six inch Buck locking in, and it meant different things to different people. It meant I was dead, I knew that much without thinking.

You dumb son of a bitch, I thought, you just used up the last of your nine lives. I mean, I had been teetering on the edge of a hundred foot drop into a quarry when a dump truck almost flipped, my knee exploded when I was caught under a generator, and I've almost been crushed by a crane, but this time, I was sure my number was up. Every other time, there had been machinery failure or an operator error. This time I was the operator and this was my error. I had screwed up royally and it looked like it was time to pay the price. I was about to become one of those statistics about guys who take cold medicine or go to work drunk or drowsy so they falloff a sky scraper or get caught in machinery. At least I would be one of the most original - Contractor bludgeoned and kidnapped by four convicts who later stab him repeatedly and toss his remains in a ditch somewhere off 95. Maybe I'd get a movie of the week.

The two younger prisoners looked up at the sound of the knife and dropped the cable they were pulling. Rick was standing next to the guard and the older prisoner, who quickly stepped out of the guard's reach and moved toward me. The younger guys assessed the situation and moved toward the guard, knowing that he didn't have a gun or a chance against both of them. They didn't move quickly, but were very deliberate and calculated. If the older prisoner could get to me before the gun towers noticed anything unusual, they would have a weapon, at least one hostage, and a perfect ticket out of there. What did they have to lose? This was probably the only chance anyone of them would ever have of getting through those gates. I looked down hoping to find some way to ditch the knife. Right below me, PC, the other prisoner, and the guard were standing waiting for the rope to come back down, completely unaware of what was going on up here. If I tossed the knife, odds were the prisoner would get to it before PC and the guard. There was no way I could move fast enough to get to the ladder, or to the other side of the roof to toss the knife in the courtyard. The older prisoner was closer, fists clenched like two big boulders. From where I was kneeling on the edge of the roof, I could see the younger prisoners moving in on the guard who was backing away. He was yelling something at me as he stepped back.

"Drop it, son, goddamn it - throw it!"

Of course, he forgot to mention exactly where I should throw it. The older prisoner was only a few steps away from me, his eyes glued to the knife. Even though I could run faster scared than he could angry, my knee had me convinced I didn't even have a long shot of standing up fast, much less running. Besides, Mark was somewhere close and I wasn't sure he could pass up such a good opportunity. There wasn't much I could do and this was about the closest I'd ever been to panicking on the job.

I thought about Audrey, who when I worked late used to stay up until nine or ten, until Daddy came home, and even if I had to leave at five the next morning, she'd wake up and wave out the window to me. She'd been through enough with me not being home now and being eight she was old enough to understand why. But, she knew Daddy was always there on Saturdays, and if I had anything to stay alive for, it was her. Kneeling, absolutely defenseless, I started wondering how much of it would hurt if I jumped right then. I was about to start praying when I noticed the shadow from something very large spreading in from of me. Perfect, I thought, even if the gun tower has noticed, I'm in between the two main targets. I looked up at Mark who was hulking over me, his hands fisted at his sides. He could have knocked me flat as soon as looked at me. The older prisoner took another step and I knew he could reach me from where he stood. Mark inched forward and I could hear his breath over the rain. They stood over me for a moment, and I watched the other prisoner's mouth tighten, flatten into a snarl, his fist cocked slightly not a foot from my face.

You've done it now, asshole, was all I could think, you have done it now.

The prisoner crouched, his eyes fixing first on me, then on the knife. I took the only chance I had and stood as fast as I could. I felt more than saw him lunge at me, and leaning to the side to avoid him my leg buckled and I went down on my bad knee. Pain shot up my back and flinching I dropped the knife. It tumbled handle over blade across the slick surface of the roof. Groaning and trying to move, I squinted up to see Rick hauling ass down the ladder like one of those cartoon characters who didn't have to deal with gravity. The other prisoners saw the knife sliding across the roof, now fair game, and took their chance at the guard who stopped backing up and turned to follow the hot trail Rick had burned down the ladder. I struggled to stand, expecting to feel a blade at my back. Turning, I saw Mark standing between my knife and the prisoner who had tried to jump me. He kicked the Buck back towards me, the wooden handle stopping with a thump against my steel-tipped boot.

"Put your knife away."

I looked up at Mark in disbelief. He stood rigid, his arms crossed, facing off with the other prisoner. He had every chance in the world to get on the right side of those gates, to get out of the hell he was living. I knew he had nothing to lose and I couldn't move, just couldn't. Without taking his eyes off the other prisoner, Mark said, "If I'd have wanted your knife, I'd have taken it while we were sitting in the truck. Put it away and do your work. These guys won't bother you any."

The younger two prisoners had moved back and stood near the ladder. The older man took a few steps back, his eyes still fixed on my knife as if he would try getting through Mark if he had half a chance. I reached down, unlocked the blade, and snapped the buck back into its sheath on my belt. One of the guards who had been left to watch the gate was just scaling the ladder, his radio in hand, followed by PC, who had more heart than he had brains. From where we were on the roof I could see the Warden storming across the courtyard, gesturing wildly toward the roof, his tie trailing loosely from his neck. My knees were shaking and I hadn't really figured out that I wasn't dead, but I was glad that what ever happened hadn't hurt too badly.

When everything quieted down, Rick, PC and I finished pulling what little cable was left and hooked up the generator. I was working in a kind of daze, not even feeling my knee anymore, just doing what had to be done. I couldn't keep my mind off what had happened, and I kept hearing my knife locking in, seeing Mark standing over me in the rain. I wasn't really sure how to thank him,

I mean, how do you say, "Hey, thanks for not killing me, man. That was mighty nice of you." Mark had just stood there like nothing had happened. Last I saw him, he was walking in a line with the other prisoners, flanked by three guards who were escorting them back to their cells. I never did ask him why he was there.

I know there was no excuse for getting on the roof with my knife. I could put it up to lack of sleep, fatigue, but the truth is I just flat out forgot where I was. I was at work and that's all that was on my mind right then. Like I've always said, when a man makes a mistake like that, you can judge him by the quality of the lesson he's learned or the quality of his eulogy. Luckily, I got the lesson this time. It's something I think about driving past Marley Station on the way to the shop, thinking it's funny how the world passes Mark by because he's a prisoner of the state, and passing me by because I'm prisoner of a state of mind. It's something I think about on Friday nights, sitting at the bar across the river, out of the shop but still on call, and I think, I finally got that life I've been asking for, now what the hell am I going to do with it? I think about it when I pick up Audrey and she's at the window, 8:30 sharp every Saturday morning, and I think how some things aren't worth losing. I think about it when there's no workmen and it's just me, and I think how we don't always take the chances we're given.

Fire Dancing

Alyssa Milletti

Janie was slowly coming undone.

To make matters worse, she was seeing a married man. Not married for long though, Janie thought. Peter had told his wife he wanted a divorce. "Well what did you go and do that for?" Janie whined. Sharing someone's husband had only entitled her to half a man. Even less. She hadn't wanted this. A whole man? All to herself? What would she do with him? And as she listened, again, to how Carol had dropped a bottle of wine, red splattering everywhere, Peter nestled his head into her lap and ... began to weep uncontrollably. Crying, he said, because he was mourning his failed marriage and feeling guilty for leaving the children. Crying, Janie knew, because he wanted to take her to bed but was sure she'd say no.

It wasn't until she met him that she realized how lonely she'd been. He was a warm body to sleep next to. So, when he kissed her, she kissed him back, offering him the passion his marriage was supposedly lacking and the under- standing he thought he deserved. And they could talk. About his wanting to quit the mutual funds corporation he worked for and write children's stories. And how she found, at the awkward age of twelve, how a camera could express her anger at her father's sudden death and her mother's subsequent nervous breakdown. Had she been home, this would've never happened, but she was here, alone. Everything new and uninviting.

But she couldn't stand the guilt festering inside her any more - she was a thief. As the divorce became finalized, she became more and more disgusted with herself, but she blamed Peter instead. Every touch, every kiss, made her shudder. And he noticed.

She couldn't deal with him. Not tonight. Tonight she needed to breathe. She needed to think. Needed him gone. And with a few tender embraces and warm kisses on his neck, she lovingly pushed him over the threshold and closed the door.

It was past midnight and the dark bags under her eyes told her she - needed sleep. Instead she cleaned, trying to organize something in her life. She scrubbed until her eyes watered from bleach and her nose burned with ammonia. She labeled everything: boxes of scrap paper, envelopes or credit card receipts, tin foil covering half-eaten food, bags for stockings with runners. She alphabetized her CDs, tapes, and videos. She color coordinated her closet and drawers. She even re-arranged her books in size order. And finally she fell down exhausted, as the sun rose across an orange sky.

"What are you doing?" Peter demanded on his next visit.

"What are you doing?" She threw back at him as she stared out the living room window. He was talking about the apartment's pungent smell of Lysol. She was talking about Carol and the kids.

He said he didn't understand what had been going on for the last few \ months, but that she was the one. Could she remember that?

One what? Janie thought.

The phone was ringing and Janie reached out from under the warmth

of her covers, feeling for the receiver.

"Hello," the frog in her throat croaked.

"Hello," the voice echoed back.

"Who is this?" she asked, clearing her throat.

"Who's this?" the voice demanded.

"This is Janie," she said annoyed, "Who are you?"

"Is anyone there?" The voice sounded concerned. "Hello. Hello?"

Janie heard a click.

"We should talk like this more often," she said perturbed, slamming down the phone. She thrust her head under her pillows and screamed. Eventually she fell back asleep, mumbling about what kind of crazy person would call before eight.

Emmy was asleep when Janie stopped by to see her. Just looking at her, peaceful and in bed, Janie felt some sort of relief from what was eating her from the inside out. Emmy was a resident of Shady Hills Retirement Community, where Janie worked. She had first seen Emmy screaming at one of the head nurses; something about wanting more rice pudding. She was a fiery old woman with big hair and big breasts who only let people she liked to call her Emmy, instead of Emily. Janie had watched with intensity as the old woman took charge of the situation, despite being in a wheelchair. She liked Emmy right away. She liked Emmy a whole lot.

Later that evening, during a break, Janie had found her room. Emmy had been anything but cordial, arguing that Janie's present of extra rice pudding was a sympathy gift.

"I am not dead yet," she had barked at Janie, "so don't think I need pity from the likes of you." Emmy planned everything, and death wasn't in her calendar any time soon.

Janie began to eat the rice pudding, dipping her index finger into the container and then sucking the pudding off with a loud, slurping noise. She was hoping to annoy the crazed bat in front of her.

"Look, you don't want this. Fine. But if you don't calm down, I'll tell that nurse you were yelling at today that you stole it," Janie said calmly, smirking at Emmy as she stuck her finger back into the pudding. If she can't accept someone being nice to her, that's her problem, she thought.

"Blackmail?" Emmy questioned, astonished. She liked this girl. She . wasn't like the rest of the idiots working at Shady Hills.

Janie nodded confidently, "I'm not getting in trouble for missing rice pudding."

Emily was silent for a moment and then pointed at her top desk drawer." There's silverware in there. Get two spoons and for the love of God, stop sticking your dirty fingers in my dessert," she commanded, warming up a bit. "So, what's your name?" she asked. Janie told her. "Janie," she said it out loud to herself, "well, it will have to do. You call me Emmy, okay?"

Peter was here, in her cramped apartment. It wasn't as nice as the first one Janie had rented. But when her photos stopped selling she was forced to move. They began arguing while she was showing him some new photos she'd developed and they were arguing still, while they did the dishes. She hadn't meant to start a fight; it was only supposed to have been a hypothetical - question. She needed to know how he'd react if she made their we a you and me. But she knew, before that occurred, she'd have to find the courage to be alone again. To start over by herself.

"You know, I met this boy at work today. Mrs. D'Angelo's nephew? He asked me out on a date." There had been no boy and she didn't know any D' Angelos.

"Oh," he said, handing her another dish. "That's nice. Will you be going?" Peter was worried, unable to figure out why she was being so casual about this. This was the woman he was leaving his wife for.

Taking the dish, she replied, "I was thinking about it. Do you think I should go?" She couldn't believe how calm he was being, considering he was leaving his wife for her.

"I think," he looked at her from the corner of his eye, "you think for yourself and you'll make the right decision." He wanted to wrap his arms around her and tell her to say no. But if there was one thing he'd learned about Janie, if someone tells her not to do something, she'll want to do it even more.

"Is there a right decision?" Janie took the stack of clean dishes and put them in the cabinet above the oven.

"Isn't there?"

She sat down at the kitchen table, the wicker chair creaking under her weight. "So, hypothetically speaking, what would you do if I said yes?" She was digging for an answer, almost hoping he'd blow up.

"Hypothetically speaking?" He threw a towel over his left shoulder and looked at her.

"Is there any other way?"

"I'd say I'd feel betrayed."

She crossed her arms and snorted. "I think that's a load of hypothetical crap." She was annoyed at his lack of concern but was even more agitated by the "betrayed" comment. Betrayed, to Janie, inferred some sense of loyalty. What am I? A dog?

Peter went into the hallway closet and pulled out a long gray raincoat and golf umbrella.

Janie called from the kitchen, "Can I ask you another hypothetical question?" Her pride had been stung and she wanted to kill the bee.

"Could I possibly stop you?" He called back. This was getting out of hand. She was starting to remind him of the girls.

"Good form, ol' chap," she laughed in her best Cockney accent. "What would you do if I sent a video-tape of us to your wife?" Despite the divorce, I he still hadn't told Carol he was sleeping with another woman.

His face hardened for a moment and then relaxed. "You don't have a videotape." He slid on the raincoat.

She walked out from the kitchen with his briefcase: "That's why it's a , hypothetical question, stupid."

"Janie, where's all this coming from?" He wasn't just referring to this argument. She'd been acting strangely for months: the clothes, the photos, everything. Truth be told. Janie didn't know herself. She'd never meant to get involved with a married man. But then that's like an alcoholic saying "I never meant to be a drunk." Who grows up with Jim Beam as their hero?

The two stood in the hallway staring at each other. Peter in his raincoat and Janie in her pj's and fuzzy bunny slippers. They really were bunnies. They had pink satin ears and cotton tails behind the heels. They" stared at each other for a long time not speaking. She watched him glance at his watch, knowing what would come next.

"Janie." He was glad to leave, never having been very good at dealing with problems.

"I know. I'm still only second concubine. Go, okay?" There was no way she was putting up a fight tonight, she was too tired.

"You're beautiful. You know that?" He held her chin up in the air, analyzing her face from all angles like he would one of her photos.

She wriggled free. "So I'm told."

He kissed her on the cheek and mumbled something about his calling her.

She watched him leave and as he opened the door to walk down the stairs he turned, "Oh, and Janie? Why don't you try wearing something other than black. Okay?"

He whisked down the stairs to his other life. "I have on red socks." They were Christmas socks her mother had sent her in a care package last year. She couldn't understand why he was angry with her for this. She thought she was being practical. It's not like Christmas socks can be worn every day. She closed the door, trapped. She was having trouble leading one life. She couldn't fathom leading two.

It was true. Janie had taken to wearing only black. Maybe brown or j navy on an adventurous day. It had begun by shying away from the skirts and tight pants in her closet, opting for black jeans and oversized sweaters instead. She wanted to hide herself, figuring that if she couldn't see her body, nobody else could either. She couldn't attract any more fathers. So she gave almost all of her brightly colored clothing to the Salvation Army.

Closing the door, Janie stopped and stared at herself in the hallway mirror. Her body was wilted. Her stomach withdrawn, concave. Her arms reminded her of tentacles - long and limp; hanging at her sides. Her collar bone jutted out of her skin. She poked at her sunken cheeks and softly sang, "Peter, Peter, pumpkin eater." She knew he was worried about her. He would grow quiet and sullen, furrow his brow, and eventually moan, "Oh, Janie. What are you doing?" "How sweet," she would sigh, kissing him quickly on the cheek and then fluttering away "you love me. You really love me." And he did.

"You know what you are? You're a home wrecker. And I am not friends with any home wreckers," Emmy said angrily, looking out the window.

Janie whined, "Aw, Emmy. Come on."

"No. I won't come on," she stumbled," you're a beautiful girl. You're a talented girl. I don't know what it is that you're getting from him, but whatever it is, it's not any good," she raised her voice, "and I don't think you should be a part of it. You know what I always say..."

"I know, Emmy, I know," she interrupted, bored by the nagging. And they said in unison, "Sometimes the princess would be better off saving herself."

They were both quiet for a moment, holding each other's hands; \ intertwining smooth, milky flesh with wrinkles and veins. "Emmy," she asked quietly, "what if the princess can't save herself?"

Emmy stroked Janie's hair and replied lovingly, "Then she comes here and we talk about it over rice pudding."

Janie was erasing another prank message from her answering machine, as she looked through her mail which was sitting in a pile on the wooden, antique table by the front door. There was a postcard from her mother in Malibu.

> *Sweetheart,*
> *Having a blast. Wish you were here. Hope everything is going well with Peter. Why don't you two come out for a while and join me? We haven't seen each other in so long. I miss my Tweety-bird.*

Past Work Experiences

James Palma

To Whom It May Concern:

Based on the small space allotted for job experience on this application, I am enclosing an extra sheet in order to adequately list and explain my past work experience. I apologize for the length, but I feel that it will be much more accurate if I explain these jobs than if you call these former "employers" for information.

1986-1987   Now Playing Video

Being my first job, I found my experience at Now Playing to be quite an exciting one. As the only person from Eastern High working at a video store, I was nearly elevated to celebrity status, as I'm sure you can imagine. Suddenly everyone was my friend, and everyone loved to come and visit me in the store. However, store owner Bill Brennan was not a very amiable man, and threatened to fire me after walking in on one of my in-store showings of "Dirty Dancing" that I liked to hold for my friends. He was very angry about this, but I'm sure he wasn't so concerned about the chairs that I had set up as he was jealous of the beauty and grace of Patrick Swayze, who is featured so prominently in the film. His inability to listen to reason was truly unveiled when I was fired after being accused of renting free videos to my (then) best friend Missy. This was an unfounded accusation, however, as there is a fine line between free and "borrowed." However, I do not want to bore you with a lot of video store industry jargon, so I will move on.

1987-1987 Common Grounds Coffee

Thoroughly disgusted with my video experience, I decided to try my hand at the world of coffee brewing. By far the biggest surprise for me at this job was learning that shops like this open at 5 am each morning, something that they forgot to put on their job application. Luckily, the owner Rich and I eventually came to an agreement that it would be in our best interest if I only work the late shift, as my early morning grogginess had led to a freak coffee grinder accident which ; nearly took the fingers of a customer. (Again, I will spare you the coffee industry jargon of the story and move on). My move even opened up a space for my (ex) best friend Missy to work the early shift, which I felt very good about as Missy is a little slow and sometimes has trouble getting jobs. But most importantly, it gave me a chance to meet Mark Delano. Yes, I was hypnotized by Mark Delano, with his curly hair, chubby little hips, and eyes that I swear looked like I the Columbia Supremo beans that were on special the day that we met. Our relationship brewed faster than that day's house blend, and before I knew it I was in love. We spent all of our time together, in and out of work. Unfortunately, I soon lost my job at the shop. After winning tickets on KC 101 (I was on the radio!) to see Bon Jovi, I begged Rich to give me the night off. He wouldn't budge, though, and I'll be damned if Richie Sambora would come to my town without me seeing him. I went to

the concert, and lost my job the next day, which on reflection is a good thing since I truly was not being challenged
brewing coffee all day.

1987-1987 Friendly's Restaurant

A new Friendly's had just opened up, giving me the opportunity to find employment very quickly after Common
Grounds fell through. This job soon turned out to be a
terrible choice, as by the end of my first night I ended
up tired and grumpy, with ice cream smeared allover my
shirt and arms. (What their application fails to tell you
is that you not only have to serve tables, but you have
to clean them as well. Slavery, anyone?). My father, who
I'm sure is on a quest to ruin my life, came in for dinner
the first night and took pictures of me as I waited on his
table. Half the school is in the place, and he starts taking
pictures. So, for the first time, I left a job without being
asked to leave. I just threw my apron at my father and
walked straight out and drove to Mark's. Dad wasn't too
happy, I but he has to learn somehow that I am a mature
adult, not just his little 16 year old daughter.

1987-1987 Ashley's Ice Cream

Feeling confident in the food service business, I moved
on to ice cream. 'Luckily Mark and I were able to keep
in touch- I missed him terribly, but knew that our { love
for each other would withstand our separation. Things
seemed to be going well, that is until that fateful March
night when Missy came .str~"ing in hand in I
hand WIth none other than Mark! What a surprise she
got, thinking that I wasn't working that night. It turned

out that Missy took the late shift when I left the coffee shop, and her and Mark found love somewhere between the dessert rack and the espresso maker. And she thought that she could get away with it. Stupid Missy Orlando! Missy, who could barely spell her own name, not to mention get a job without my help. And Mark, pudgy little Mark, who I thought I found love in. What I never told him was that he smelled—he really did. No matter what he did there was always this strange beef-vegetable soup odor to him. Despite my shock, I felt like I handled the situation much better than they did. They only stood there, tubby and the mental midget, at a loss for words. So I decided to break the silence, and said, "How about a banana split guys, or are you saving that for when you're alone later on?" Well, I thought Missy was going to pass out, and Mark had to practically carry her out (not without shouting some very hurtful words to me which wouldn't be appropriate to include here). Unfortunately, I was fired the next day, as I got very depressed after they left and went though nearly a gallon of Rocky Road while blasting Eric Carmen's masterpiece "All by Myself" throughout the store repeatedly.

1987-?? McDonald's (Hopefully!)

OK, I know that you haven't hired me yet for this job, but since I feel so confident that I could succeed here, I thought that I would include this anyway. Some of my "friends" at school think that it is funny that I have a desire to put on a paper hat and work the french-fry broiler. However, it is a responsibility that I look forward to greatly. Growing up, I have spent much time at this fine restaurant, and I feel like I can give something back. Before Missy became an evil traitor we would spend hours here, passing the time with a Big Mac or milkshake. It is a place where I feel at home, and could succeed. The fact that Missy has succeeded in turning many of my friends against me has freed up much of my time, so flexibility will be one of my strong points. Finally, I feel that my past work experience has turned me into a mature person (much more mature than some- one like Mark or Missy). I ask you to take all of this into consideration as you read this application, and I look forward to hearing from you soon.

Ordinary Time
Katie McHugh

There is nothing outside my apartment window except an ordinary, quiet street far below. My watch reads two minutes past three, which makes him officially late—boyfriends always are. I know that I know exactly where James is. Exasperated nonetheless, my hands jump into my combed hair, involuntarily twisting it into a knot at the nape of my neck.

My apartment, like the street, is unusually empty for a Saturday. The living room couch is gone. I went discount furniture shopping last week and found an adorable, navy plaid couch: firm, comfortable, matches the room's color scheme. It was ordered, charged, and supposed to have come by Thursday. It hasn't. My deteriorated beige sofa—a lumpy relic from my college dorm—I've already donated to the local youth center, and two teenage boys in sweat-stained t-shirts hauled it away yesterday. Impatient, I dance to the center of the small room, do a half-pirouette in my delicate dress and inappropriate shoes, and the collapse on the rug, my elbow propped against the narrow mahogany coffee table. The corner lamp isn't pretty in the daytime when it's turned off; the shade looks dull. Wallpaper needs to go one of these days. And the floor is hard beneath my mated carpeting. Where's the couch? I called UPS yesterday and they actually tracked it to Milwaukee.

The air is dusty and dim, except for bands of afternoon sunlight streaking faded walls and sagging ceiling. I arch my back against the table, listening to the hum of the world, straining to hear a car slowing, an engine stopping. We're supposed to have an early dinner, but first we're going to visit my mother at the St. Joseph's Church Bazaar, where she's hand-beading rosaries. Seven minutes late.

But the buzzer bleats. I'm not going to go crazy in my half-naked living room after all. Rather than wait for him to trek up three flights of stairs, or wait for an elevator that will never arrive, I gather myself up like a pile of clothing, thrown in the direction of the door, and the rush to meet him.

We bump into each other in the lobby, really a poorly protected cubicle of space separating the building's elevators form the sidewalk, with a vacant desk and two potted rubber plants.

"Sorry I'm late," his mouth offers a shy smile, as he pushes the glass doors open. "I was at the program this morning."

"I know," I sigh, and we step towards his old car.

I work as a legal secretary and attend a second-rate graduate school for writing of all other things: James is a financial analyst for a Cincinnati law firm and a professional volunteer, so I like to explain. He is taller, and a year older, mild, usually looking as though he'd rather think about you than talk to you.

Polished burgundy loafers, dark belted jeans and a green polo shirt. He's wearing his new glasses. Last Saturday we went to the eyeglass place in the mall to pick out frames. The woman behind the counter – a mass of frizzy hair and a boxy, flowery dress—suggested a black frame of medium thickness. "These are German glasses," she chuckled. "They make everyone who wears them look German. You'll look German!"

He tried them on and I liked them, so he bought them. James is half-Italian and half-Scottish, but the pitch worked. The glasses match his dark hair and light complexion nicely.

James volunteers weekends at the Dorothy Day House, the city's soup kitchen, serving balanced breakfasts and sandwiches. I've worked a few times; the though of going more often feels guilty to me. It's a small brick building on the other side of Cincinnati, stained with graffiti, although the interior is kept immaculate. The plain cream colors, flickering fluorescent bulbs, long, fake-wooden folding tables and orange plastic chairs all remind me of my grade school cafeteria, complete with name-stickered, gray-haired monitor ladies. The patrons are usually interesting to talk to. A few weeks ago, one man wearing a ski jacket and a jack o'lantern grin, between sips of coffee, explained to me his theory on religion. It was all about love, he said, too big to explain, like the universe, like God; God just lets the universe go, and sometimes Satan tries to snatch it away, you see? I saw, I said. He stared at me with wide brown eyes that left deep creases in his temples when he blinked. "Your eyes," he decided slowly, "are like the cosmos."

We're driving, weaving out of bottled-up lanes and into deceptively clear ones. Now we're stopped at a light and poised to make an illegal turn, and I point this fact out. James is preoccupied, smoking a cigarette out the window.

"How many are you down to now?"

"Two a day."

"Two?"

"Maybe three. I have a lot on my mind," he sighs, letting the exhausted cigarette fly towards the pavement.

James is driving one-handed and that scares me. When he's distracted, he fumbles with his glasses, the mirrors, his buttons, focusing too much attention on the radio dial and not enough on the road. The last time he had a lot on his mind he was worried about the health of a middle-aged woman who lives at the shelter, and ran the car into a streetlight post while searching for an a.m. radio advice show.

He settles on a new station that sounds as if it's blasted out of 1948. Glancing over, he notices my right hand, knuckles white from clutching the door handle. "I'm alright," he grins baby milk teeth at me. "How was your day?"

"Great; no couch," I tell him. James nods, his pale, square jaw moving steadily. His face is clean-shaven. I have a bad habit of staring at nose profiles and ears and sideburns when someone is trying to concentrate on driving straight.

"No couch," he frowns, contemplating this for a moment.

"None," I say. He's not being very talkative today; I haven't even heard one Dorothy Day story yet, and we've been traveling for fifteen minutes. I lean back and lay my head in the crevice between the car door and my seat, listening to the tragic news of the world buzzing and fading when we drive under overpasses, fireflies of sound dying in a jar.

By the time we arrive at the church, the lot is full and cars are haphazardly parked all over the grass. It looks more like a carnival; children are bouncing and shouting on a giant air-castle, smoke is billowing from barbecue grills, and balloons are escaping left and right. "You and James have to come," my mother begged me on the phone the night before. "Proceeds go to the renovations!" My mother has recently been appointed to St. Joseph's building committee, in charge of fundraising, expanding the church. Towards the rectory I can see rows of crepe-paper covered tables, various knickknacks perfect for …well, perfect for supporting a good cause anyway. Somewhere in the crowd, my mother is seated in a metal folding chair, laughing and smoothing her hair in the wind, chatting with Fr. Foley and hawking rosaries at the same time.

After walking around for a few minutes, everything suddenly feels more normal. Parents are roping in their children, ice cream is melting on the blacktop, rainbows are painted on almost translucent cheeks. "Want a balloon?" James kids. "No," I tease back, "I want a goldfish." A Boy Scout troop is having a sale about twenty feet away.

"You got it," he laughs, walking over to the table. I grab his arm. "I don't really want one," I say, but it's too late. The wallets out and he's buying me a two-dollar goldfish in water in a bulging plastic bag. It's heavy and dangerous. The fish's eye is dilated and bewildered.

"Maybe I'll write a story about this fish," I muse.

"Don't drop it," he cautions. "You'll have to call it 'a fish out of water.'"

"Ha-ha-ha," I exaggerate.

James looks sly. "You should write about a boat."

"A boat?"

"I have a story for you: a boat, and it sinks. It hits an iceberg and it sinks. It's a tragedy."

My face breaks into a smile. "Maybe there could be a lot of people on the boat. Maybe my story will be really popular and I can turn it into a movie."

"There you go," he says. "It could be an epic. Make sure you include several nudity scenes, though."

"Oh, I will…Seriously though. I need a story: An idea."

"I told you, write an epic. You could write the next *Odyssey*."

"It's been done. That was *Ulysses*."

He laughs a gruff German-sounding laugh. "I'll call you Joyce, then," he says, taking my hand.

We find my mother. Though her hands are folded on the rosary table, she's not hard to miss with the dyed platinum hair that clashes with her age. She thinks she's trendy in that bright outfit, but now—I view it objectively even in this crowd—it's still just an old-lady floral dress. She giggles at my fish, which I carry gingerly, a water balloon ready to burst at my feet if I make one clumsy move. She starts telling me a "can you believe this?" story about the rudeness of a lady in her sewing circle, and James is leading on the table, crinkling the paper, talking with Fr. Foley. A breeze drifts by and it occurs to me that for the first time this week, the sun is out, ripening through the trees, blanketing our tables white and warming our shoulders. We lounge for half an hour. James buys a rosary from my mother before we go. I thought he was just doing it to be nice.

We won't have dinner until 6 o'clock. We're late again, stuck between exits on the highway because a car cut too close to a tractor-trailer. For half an hour we have no idea why traffic is at a dead stop; even the up-to-the-minute radio broadcast has yet to cover the story. All we see are a barrage of ambulances and police cars are plowing through the emergency lane. All we hear are sirens approaching and wailing away: jarring, unpopular music.

I'm driving now, and only get a brief view of the wreck as we inch forward and finally pass it. James is gawking behind the window glass, jaw set to cringe, as though he is looking at a terrifying museum exhibit. News helicopters are chopping overhead and the radio is now providing the historical summary.

"…and on I-75 a terrible, fatal three car accident—Oh that's awful, Les—Sure is, Samantha…Anyone traveling southbound on I-75 should find an exit, because heavily backed-up traffic is only beginning to clear...Police say one driver was trying to pass a tractor-trailer...One passenger has died and three others are being rushed to St. Luke's Hospital..."

I glance longer than I should. The area is sectioned off by flares, shouts and flashing police lights. Lots of guys in uniforms, mustaches and sunglasses, are busy, directing traffic and leaning into small, hand-held radios. The trailer is perched perilously between a broken guardrail, cliff and highway. A red car is flipped over in the embankment, grounded in tall weeds. A third car, a white one, is on the shoulder of the highway, slightly dented. The innocent bystander, traveling in the right lane when a car and a truck came swooping over. There is a huddle around the injured, so I can't see any blood, or a body bag, or whatever my riveted eyes have hoped to see. And then we're by—we're passed.

The atmosphere is numbing. We're driving through a tunnel of trees, following a dotted white line as usual. "How's the fish," I finally say, looking straight ahead.

In my peripheral view, James has his palm on top of the bag, as if he is covering the fish's eyes. "Oh... it's fine," he replies belatedly, still starring out the window. Right now he's thinking of death and pain, life and peace, and a telephone call from God, of things I will not know about until we have our own fatal accident, dinner at the Sweetwater Café.

There is no wait at the bright, eclectically decorated restaurant. James has his arm around me and is rubbing my shoulder, as if trying to melt away the inexplicable tension between us. Sensing his nervousness makes my own mind wander.

A string of rehearsed words leaves his mouth the moment we sit in the cushioned chairs. "We need to talk…I need to tell you this now," he sighs, eyes looking away from underneath his black glasses, and then suddenly I know we won't be discussing hunger programs or homeless shelters.

"You know that I love you," he says. What? Oh, God. This is it; this is the line. I close my eyes briefly; I want to plug my ears the way children do. One year, one month, six days, eighteen hours, destination: breakup.

"I've been thinking about this for a long time, for about six months, and lately I've been sure, and now I'm really sure." He clears his throat. "I don't think I'm cut out to be an analyst. Or to work at a firm."

My shoulders collapse with temporary relief. "All right then," my face relaxes.

"Because I've been called," he continues. His fingers drumming the tablecloth.

I don't understand yet. "Who called you?" I'm wary now, and angry, expecting to hear an ex-girlfriend's name.

"I mean, I have a calling. I know I'm not making any sense. This is just so hard for me to tell you." Another deep sigh, pregnant pause, peak of drama.

"I'm thinking of entering the seminary."

This is the part where everything is slow motion and rapid pace all at once. Shock. Lean forward. Sit back. Clutch a fork. "A sem-in-ary? You're going to be a priest. A Catholic priest?"

He takes off his glasses to rub his eyes, upset that I'm upset. "I think so," he whispers. "I know that is what I'm called to do. I want to help people. I want to understand them, and listen to them. And—the accident today—seeing the accident today made me feel so helpless. Although that's not what made me decide, although I guess it did finally inspire me to decide, but really, but no, I just think it was a sign from God, that I'm choosing the right path. I need to do this, to have peace with myself."

He's not looking at me. I'm dizzy with the illogic of the statements. I want to say can't you help people without being a priest? You do help people now. You help hundreds of people now. You help me now. Can't you you can't can't can't. But I remain quiet. I drink my whole glass of water, trying to keep a steady occupation in the chaos, trying, at the same time, not to choke.

Obviously, it's over. Just like that, we're over. Two hours ago, buying a goldfish together; now, goldfish has a broken home. Did I cause this? Is this me? He says no. He doesn't think so. My lip is raw from biting it. I could make a scene, yelling and screaming about how selfish he is and tip the table into his lap. I could dump his water glass on his head. But wait, you can't throw a glass at a priest, because priests aren't selfish! What a nasty, horrible breakup trick! The blood ebbs form my face and I won't plead temporary insanity; dignity is the best choice. A dignified response will prove how supportive I am. "I see. I understand. I mean, I don't understand, but maybe I can understand. I don't know." I drop my napkin onto the table. "I think I'd like to go home now."

"I understand," he nods solemnly. He's already solemn. He leaves a tip for the befuddled waiter, who hasn't even brought us salads yet. I haven't eaten anything after all, anything besides a glass of water and an ice cube. The water is sloshing around in my trembling stomach, which is confused, empty, and longing for the signal of substance.

There's nothing worse than, having been dumped by your boyfriend in the name of the Lord, inadvertently deadbolting and un-deadbolting your door when you're trying to get inside and falling onto the couch that isn't there. "God damn fucked-up fuck!" I mutter. My pantyhose are ripped and my knee has a brush burn. Answering machine silent: no messages. Letterbox: no mail. My blue sofa love-seat is still in Milwaukee, well across the state line, and the space in my living room irritates me, haunting the apartment like the unshakable, prickly feeling of a phantom limb.

The oblivious goldfish has managed to survive the trip, resting safely on the floor, in his water-baggie home still intact. He floats quietly to the bottom, fins barely whispering movement. Frustrated, I search my cabinets for an empty Mason jar and scoop up the bag, pick the plastic knot and pour the fish inside. I add a cup of water; bubbles rise to the surface. The fish appear slightly unsettled but adapts to the new habitat. I give him a pinch of complementary fish food and stare into the green-tinted jar. For a moment, I consider dumping its entire contents down the toilet.

Every time I see my reflection in the bathroom mirror I remind myself to get rid of fluorescent bulbs. Between the lights, the dry air, worn-off powder, and trauma-induced blotchiness, my skin is a pink mess, like a healing sunburn victim's. Where is my concealer? I make myself up again to regain some sense of decency. I am dignified.

As my reflection wavers in the mirror, the phone summons. I spring to answer it, bounding across the carpet and over my kicked-off shoes, both praying and fearing who it could be. It's not; the voice belongs to my friend Carrie.

"What are you up to tonight?"

"Nothing." For once, it is the absolute truth.

"Let's go to bar, girls' night," she prods.

My heads are unsteady and pale, and the thought of beer in my empty stomach makes me wince. But I'm too dazed to make decisions and too angry to protest getting drunk. "All right," I agree. "I'll meet you at nine." We always go to the same bar, The Cove. It's half a block away from my building.

It's cooler out now and I'm wearing a black short-sleeved dress, new stockings to cover up my swelling, blue-black knee. Instant goosebumps, hair standing straight up, like a thousand thin, tiny dog's ears, pricked at a faint sound—that's the soul of me. Cars are drifting between traffic lights. Clusters of teenage girls come and go. On the right are two more apartment buildings and a deli, the neon sign illuminating the vicinity more than other streetlights. Across the street is the Episcopal Church, a gray stone castle with three neddlelike steeples. The bell is not ringing, thank God. My feet pause approaching it. Will this sight, this monstrous, gloomy giant, finally register enough ugliness to stir my nerves and make me cry?

The patches of sidewalk in front of the church are empty, the heavy gothic wooden doors are closed, and the walk sign is lit pale green. I could go in. I could pray. Pray that James stops being an idiot. He could have become an Episcopal minister, couldn't he? Same vestments, same sacraments, girlfriend included? Aren't Episcopals just Catholics with common sense? They have women priests; some factions are even hoping for homosexuality to be tolerated in a rational, timely way—they live in the real world. But I can't compete: James want to marry the Lord, not me. I walk on, allowing the church to drop farther and farther behind.

I can hear the insistent bass thump when I'm ten feet away. The Cove takes up the next corner block; flashes of light blink where the black curtains covering the tall windows do not meet. "Hi, Bill," I sigh to the bouncer, a thick, muscular man in a crew cut and too-tight black shirt. "Hey," his chin protrudes.

The bar is cramped. Herds of people are scrunched together at tables meant for two; crammed body-to-body on a tiny slab of a dance floor; clamoring around a lone pool table. I meander over to a vinyl stool and order and order a double shot. A knocked-over beer bottle is dripping a steady pool on the floor near the legs of my stool. I nudge the seat to the left. The stool makes an uncomfortable scraping noise.

I eye the doorway. Carrie—where the fuck is she? My trauma is going stale; it needs telling or it might curdle. An attractive bartender shoves my double-shot in front of me, and I drink it, before I can worry whether or not it's impolite to not wait for the guest. My throat harbors a stale burn and my insides a warm, mollifying feeling.

A blond man I vaguely recognize (the bus stop? James' apartment complex?) is sitting at the other end of the bar. He is dressed casually, and when he moves his wrist the silver band of his watch flickers. I cross and uncross my legs and pull my hair in front of my shoulders. When he shifts in my direction, I smile the daring smile.

As planned, he sidles over. "Can I buy you a drink?"

It's 9:09 and Carrie isn't here. "Sure," I say with a false brightness. Jesus, going to be plastered before Carrie even slings her purse on a damp bar. I'm sticking with hard liquor tonight so he orders a Long Island Iced Tea for me, and a beer for himself. "I've seen you somewhere," he says loudly, over the din. "I can't remember where, though."

I'm glad the impression is mutual. "Yes, you look familiar," I admit. The drinks are on the counter and I'm guzzling amiably.

"So, come here often?" he attempts. I'm holding a steady buzz and he has nice teeth, so I'm willing to forgive the cheap line. "Yeah, what's your sign," I giggle. Oops.

I didn't mean to say that.

"Virgo," he says, not noticing the unintended tinge of sarcasm in my voice. "Virgo," I echo. Suddenly Madonna pop enters my head: 'Like a virgin-ooh-touched for the very first time…'

"What do you do?"

"I'm in grad school, a writer," I announce importantly. At least, I would be if I had a story or poem half-finished on a disk somewhere. "What do you do?"

Now he's talking about investing or something and I'm inquiring about 401K plans; I'm not sure how we arrived at this topic. There's nothing funnier than a fledging writer pretending to know about money. Time to flirt. "Time for another drink?" I ask. "How about martini's?" At this point I've forgotten about Carrie, and it appears that she's forgotten about me too. Nowhere in sight.

His name is Derek ad he's not bad looking—thin nose, somewhat muscular build. I'm sure I could pick him up. I have picked him up; I could carry him home now if I wanted to. It occurs to me that James will never sleep with anyone--- we were waiting until marriage, so he said—and that abrupt thought startles me. "Don't be a priest," I tell Derek, wide-eyed and in a serious voice.

He looks puzzled but I keep babbling on. "It's terrible thing to give up your whole life for. I mean, maybe when your thirty, thirty-five, and have lived a little bit, then if your single, and want spiritual fulfillment, ok, maybe. But, God, it seems like such a waste!"

"I don't want to be a priest," he confides, bemused. Now is the moment where eh should state that he has someone to meet, or that gosh it's late and he has someplace to be. Yet, he just sips his martini and waits for me to go on.

"Oh, I know you don't," I laugh, as though the idea

is hilarious. "But I'm just saying, I know I read somewhere that even though the Catholic population is hugely increasing, the number of priests are decreasing. Those priests are all getting older and every year fewer and fewer men wander toward the seminaries. It's practically helpless. It's practically a lost cause. So what is going to happen when the day comes and there aren't any more priests, and then suddenly Catholicism, the biggest fucking denomination in America, is over! Finished! What's going to happen then? What does that mean? What does that say about religion at all?" I'm out of breath and out of martini. I slump back against the edge of the bar, trying to remember where I am, who I am, and everything I just said.

"Wow." He runs his fingers through his blond hair. "That's something to think about, I suppose."

"Yeah, well you know, it's all celibacy," I rush on. "When forced to choose, most people are going to pick sex over religion. Because, sex isn't a bad thing. Especially, if, say, you're in love."

"Hmmm," he frowns, and then smiles again, inching closer to me. I've at least introduced some subjects he's got some allegiance and sympathy to. His hand is on my sore knee. "Do you want to dance?"

"Dance?" I'm confused. I don't see what dancing has to do with any this, and I'm not sure I can even stand up. "Oh. No, I can't. I'm a terrible dancer. And I need to wait for my friend. She's"—I squint at my watch—"half an hour late. At least."

"I see," he says, and his other hand lands on my hand. "Well, can I at least have your number?"

"Sure," I exhale, and rattle it off, like a schoolgirl trying to prove she knows her facts. I don't wait for him to produce a pen or a scrap of paper.

He's leaning to kiss me when I hear a name—my

name—being called in a familiar nasal tone. "Carrie!" I look up, and she's standing two feet away, gaping, at me, no, at Derek, no, at Derek clutching my palm. I'm not sure. Her hair, usually a prefect blob bob, is falling in her face. Her eyes are steely circles.

"What are you doing?" she grits her teeth at no one in particular, and then it hits me that this is the creep— Derek, Derek the creep, that Carrie dated for a month last summer. I turn back to the bar and lay my head in the counter. Carrie, taller than Derek, is pointing a red fingernail at him, as if aiming a pistol, and Derek is backing away, surrendering, pleading innocence. He's feigning confusion—motioning, as if he's not a native speaker, doesn't know the language.

"And what are you doing?" she hits my shoulder. Derek has retreated behind the pool table, pretending to be engrossed in the game. "I'm sorry," I breathe. "I didn't realize. James and I broke up today. He's going to be a fucking priest," I say matter-of-factly, as if me being dumped were a weekly phenomenon and—priests—well, that happens all the time. Or once in a while. To other people.

"A priest? What? What? Oh my God." She sits down. "Well. Well. Well. He's just gay. He must be gay." This idea, an answer, brings me back, as if even her suggestion were true, it would change something.

Gay theory. I should have known this was coming from her, who has never quite been able to get over hooking up with confessed bisexual man in college. "Thanks. Gay and celibate and dumping me. That makes me feel better."

"Oh, sweetie," she puts her arm around me, pulling to hug me, "you know that's not what I mean." And now I'm crying, four hours too late, four hours since I could have laid it on the line for James and guilt-tripped him into coming back to me. "You know what I want?" I say deliriously, my voice rising. "I want the kind of guy who spends his weekends spray painting my name on a highway overpass. That's hard work. I mean, they must have to hang upside down to write those things, and they must do it late at night, since it's gotta be illegal, the whole defacing part. That's talent! That's fucking devotion, God damn it," I sob.

Carrie is dragging me off a stool. "Good thing I got here," she reminds herself. "I have to take you home."

Carrie props me up and walks me back, even opening the door for me, relaying a complicated, apologetic story about her cat throwing up, her tape player breaking and the toilet overflowing at approximately ten of nine. There's no comfortable place to sit in my apartment anymore—my kitchen chairs are notorious, straight, rickety—so I lie down on the floor and Carrie hoists herself up onto the counter, wedging her lanky body in the space between the microwave and the refrigerator.

"You want to talk about this right now?" she asks softly.

"No." I muffle my face in the carpet.

"Ok." She pauses. "You want some water?"

"Yes," I sniff. She pours me a glass.

"Feeling better?"

"Yes," I lie. "I'm not drunk anymore." Which is physically impossible.

"Are you going to be alright?"

"Yeah. You can go if you want."

"Are you sure?"

"Yeah."

"I'll call you tomorrow, ok, hon?"

"All right." I stay sprawled out on the carpet, watching the bottom of the door open, click shut.

I want to fall asleep in my melodramatic pose, but I

can't. I'm not tired. Next to the lamp a nameless orange blur is circling the bottom of the Mason jar. I forgot to show Carrie my fish. He's finally attacking the food I left him, bits of flake dribbling form his tiny flickered mouth. I lean close to the glass, illuminated by the glow of a streetlamp outside, suck in my cheeks and make kissing noises. Puck puck puck. He's frightened and tries to dart away, but is trapped. "There's no escape," I yell.

I fumble my way into the kitchen and fill my glass again. Glug glug. The answering machine is blinking and blipping.

The first is a hang-up. The next is James.

9:05 p.m. Beep. Breathing, a deep voice. "Hello, this is God. No, hi, it's James." Odd voice, nervous joke, slightly panicked. "I need to talk to you. Are you there? Pick up the phone...hello? All right, I guess you're not there. Ok. When you get this, please call me back. I haven't changed my mind but you are a beautiful person and I love you and we need to talk about this. Call me back."

A beautiful person? Yuck. It sounds like something a priest would say to a homely person who volunteers too much. I scrunch up my face in tears again; I want to talk to him too but I can't call him drunk. You can't telephone even a pre-priests if you are wasted, thinking the thoughts I am thinking. I curse not seducing James sooner, giving him something to concrete, like a breast or a thigh to miss or ponder. But no; I was patient this time, saintly patient, and look at what it got me—a guy who thinks woo much.

I know any young priest, who's for real, who isn't gay, wants to go to some godforsaken village in South America somewhere, where the rats are as large as cats, or worse, and the air is filled with a permanent dusty cloud. They want to teach school, say mass, administer food and water- and maybe that's where James belongs.

With aspirations like that, how can he be bothered with misplaced couches? My mind is dizzy. I can't picture James's neck in a collar, but maybe him as a middle-aged man who wears one, maybe I can see that. I replay the message. "Hello, this is God. No, hi, it's James." I smile a little. Stop, click, rewind. "Hello, this is God." This is God. God, some amalgamation of Jesus. Isn't Jesus love? God!—Haven't I seen those bumper stickers?

The After Dark
Maryl Roberts

The part in my hair looked crooked in the mirror that morning, the white scalp too drastic against the brown locks. Grieving seemed to create a lack of proportion, some sense of contortion, like it unfastened your mind. I had turned the shower on as hot as I could physically bare-not hot enough to really burn. The water seemed more cleansing when it scalded. It's like taking tape to your skin, leaving it smooth, shorn.

I was standing, eyes to the sky, closed, in the midst of a shower of leaves. The whole scene reminded me of a refrigerator picture that had been passionately colored by some fierce second grader. Sliding into the white plastic lawn chair, I waited for dusk to bring light, or perhaps more literally--that obscured clarity--to a dimming day.

Looking at the white arm-rest, I wondered about the old man I saw in the store that day, hobbling around, appearing empty and lost. He smelled like cigars, wore all brown: a corduroy jacket, brown turtleneck, and what appeared to be brown polyester "slacks." His face was sweet-soft, but his smile was sad. I wondered why he was alone. I thought for a moment that perhaps he was somewhere thinking about how lonely it would be to be me, and here I am-a complete idiot-a complete loser, letting white plastic lawn chairs break my heart. Of course, I always do that, take a minuscule event and make it my own-always read too much into smile, I suppose. Even the other day when the lady behind the counter at the Uni-Mart smiled at me, I would have sworn she fell immediately in love with me, wanted to spend the rest of life with me, saw something special in me. But deep down I knew she gave that smile to everyone. That old man probably will never think about me again.

I actually made myself throw up that morning; right before I made myself go look for lawn furniture. It's funny how you take for granted being able to look at yourself. You never really understand until you do something as terrible as I did. It was not like I killed anyone, or burned down any houses, I was just selfish-and that may be the worst way to live.

Usually as I lay in my bed, trying to fall asleep, I replayed different endings to that night. Sometimes I turned away from her and smiled, just walked away into the black night. Sometimes I hugged her, held onto her blond hair, smiled, opened the door to my battered green truck and drove her home-not talking necessarily, but knowing that everything was okay. Sometimes, and this was my favorite, I left before she got there, finished my beer, took one last drag, and with a wave of my hand left the rest to party in the parking lot. We simply passed in the darkness, never knowing what harm I could cause.

Of course Mary was okay, but I was not. I saw the way people looked at me as I drove through town, or as I was stopped at the one stop light on Main Street-some looked sorry, usually friends of my mother's, like they wished they could've helped me; some looked knowing, as if they predicted my down fall from the day I was born, "Oh that Matt, I knew he wasn't right the day he came home from the hospital, always crying." Or "Well, what would did you expect-his mother left when he was in elementary school-he was bound to screw up." As if there was some kind of statistic in last month's

Good Housekeeping supporting their assertion. Most people shot a mixture of anger and disappointment at me through their eyes, making me wish I could duck my head and drive at the same time, and that hurt most of all.

She's been gone almost a year. After she left I walked around, head to the ground, apparently looking for something of substance to fill the void. I looked up the word redemption in the dictionary, thinking I had a better chance of finding it if I knew what it meant. It didn't come-or hasn't yet. Mary hasn't come back either. I see her parents every once in a while fishing in the lake right on the edge of town, sometimes I imagine that they don't know, and I'm just another guy driving by. Sometimes I think they'll ask me to join them. Or sometimes I think her father will pull out a shotgun and stare straight into my eyes-not doing anything, but making me almost want to die anyway.

Her father was one of those prominent men in the community who talked too loud, told dirty jokes when the wife wasn't around, and stood guard like a lion over his little girl. I think her mom was a hippie turned born-again-Christian. I hated the word hippie-didn't really understand it-but whatever it meant; most of them seemed to grow up to be fanatic Jesus followers. It was not a bad thing to be, I suppose-we all needed a little faith, or something to keep us together, but most of the time I think we need something more.

I went to church every morning when I was little, me, my mother, and my father-and she still left. It wasn't a bad divorce. She needed to be someone the country didn't make room for, no room between the pine trees and the flying squirrels-so she went to San Francisco--a long way from western Pennsylvania. One morning she packed her bags, made me eggs and bacon, tore apart her art studio-- shoved yarn, canvas, oil paint into her jeep, and drove away. The country felt like hands around her neck, a pillow on her face, a space with no room to dance. She had wild ideas-she could turn regular glass into a sculpture of color and light so magical you had to touch it to make sure it was real. Dad raised me-taught me to hunt, fish, and be tough. He wrapped his feelings pretty tightly around himself- liked numbers and facts better than emotion. He was the ground-she was the sky.

Whenever something bad happened, like broken bones or wisdom teeth, or when my mother missed something big like the time I pitched the no-hitter at the little league all-star game, she always sent me a piece of her stained glass. It usually worked, since it wasn't money she was sending me, or trying to buy my love with, it was time she was sending-time and love and thoughts-from thousands of miles away. I think it made my father a little jealous that she could fix things like that, but that's one of the reasons he loved her so much anyway.

So when Mary had to leave my mother sent me a stained glass sailboat-purple and yellow against a red setting sun with the words Sailor's Delight written in white calligraphy letters in the blue ocean. I hung it against the bathroom window-every time I looked at it I wanted to throw up. My mind never quite grasped why she sent me something for that occasion--or incident--or accident--or what- ever it should be called.

My father never talked about it really. He asked me if I was okay once in awhile, but he never dove too far into my heart after I told him. I knew he wanted me to grow up to be a good, honest man-and I already seemed to have ruined my chance.

* *   *   *   *

"Can you please come with me, Matt?" Ann begged. "I can't, actually, I refuse, to sit through another one of

these meetings, 'sessions whatever, by myself." The ringing phone had pulled me out of the past, pulled me out of
the lawn chair and into my shit-hole house.

"Jesus, Ann, you're always telling me how weird all
those people are-the pill poppers, the acid droppers, come
on, I've had a hell of a week." I started tracing the infinity
symbol on my dirty jeans and rocking myself back and
forth, tuning Ann out.

Ann was a recovering alcoholic, who had dabbled
occasionally in other recreational drugs-a little pot, pre-
scription drugs-nothing too hard or too often, except the
booze. We graduated from college together last May, a
local community college, and neither of us has gone too
far since then. A lot of people get sucked into small towns,
not that it's a bad thing, just a pretty bizarre phenomenon.
I often find myself making lots of comparisons between
the country and the city--especially after my mother left-
and then even more when I stayed, basically in the woods,
after graduation. I got my own place about two months
ago, but Ann still lives with her father. Sometimes I feel
like Eugene Toomer, I mean, I think he got it-I think he
got it first. The purity lies in the country side-the city is
simply one large box--imprisoning--hindering--and they
don't even realize and they don't even care, because if the
box is made of gold, the sunset against the cotton field--
or reflection in the water--means nothing.

"Matt, hell-oooh...are you still there? Come in Matt,
Come in Matt, Space Shuttle Matthew ready for landing." I was spinning around and around in the only bar
chair I have along the pseudo bar my kitchen, changing
direction every couple seconds so the phone cord didn't
wrap around too far. Ann was giggling by the time her
little space shuttle escapade was over--after much gur-
gling, blasting, and other non-identifiable noises through
the phone. Ann had a cute laugh. I smiled to myself. "Are

you coming Mr. Philosopher?" She always made jokes that I analyzed things too much--beat thoughts along the walls of my mind until they were just bloody incoherent words lying around.

"Fine, Ann, I'll go."

"Goody, Goody, Goody! Yeah!"

"Calm down dear, I'm not excited about it."

"Sure, Matt, it's like a weekly dose of entertainment if you look at it right--a bunch of freaks talking about their problems--it should make you feel better. I'll be there in five minutes." The phone went dead before I had the chance to respond.

What a feisty little thing. And little is an understatement. She's probably just barely five feet tall--almost 100 pounds, short jet-black hair--bright green eyes, porcelain skin. She's like a little doll. When Ann was in high school she could drink any football player under the table--bottles of tequila--cases of beer--just before she'd go snort a line of Ritalin. In college, it just got worse, and I found myself sucking my fingers down her throat, brushing her teeth, and sitting up beside her all night long--worried she wouldn't wake up.

One night when we were sophomores I found Ann in the bushes behind the dorms throwing up blood and singing old Bruce Springsteen songs. Her laughter covered it up the next day, making people think it was a big joke--nothing serious. Her shaking hands and unsteady eyes told a different story though.

Ann was actually the one who told me about Mary leaving. Mary got fired from the Dairy Queen the morning after it happened. Her parents didn't know for days. My stomach feels like it's eroding every time I think about that night. I knew it would be all over town by the weekend. That's what happens when you live in rural America--unless it's hunting season; no one has anything better to do than talk about what everyone else is doing. In the summer--it's even worse. In high school when Bobby stole a bottle of Jack Daniel's from his father's liquor cabinet and went cow tipping, my father told me about it before Bobby even .had a hangover. And when Stacey gave Bill a blowjob for the first time, my grandmother called me asking what the hell a blowjob was.

It happened at After Dark, when the DQ closed and we would all sit around smoking cigarettes, drinking warm beer on hot car hoods ranting about the stupid hicks who would pop up at the window during the day. Mary's told me her mother always said nothing good could happen at a place with that name. Her mother also always said that nothing good happens after mid-night. But After Dark isn't even a place really-it's just a parking lot.

So Mary's boss saw us in the field. He said it looked bad for his business. Well so did underage kids drinking beer in his parking lot. I think he just wanted Mary to himself--a young girl to sit on his lap, bring him beer, and take advantage of. She was a special girl- long blond hair, brown eyes, perfect boobs, and a great laugh. Ann and Mary were kind of friends too--even though Mary was two years behind us.

Ann's honk made me jump up--almost hurting myself--out of my old porch swing. As I walked to the car, she looked at me as if I was just having a conversation with her, not myself, as if she knew where my mind was on that porch swing. The handle was stuck on her '86 chartreuse Volvo, it always was. Reaching in through the window, my fingers found the handle and opened it from the inside. "Come on, Matt, I need to tell you something." She sounded nervous. Usually people told me to put the past in the past when they saw that look on my face--what was wrong with Ann? I took my place in the bucket seat--mended with duct tape where the leather had suffered, where time had taken its toll--I felt like it was my own bed. Leaning back, I got in the perfect position to look up at the stars. The stars were always out in small towns--I've never even seen one in a city. Once I visited Baltimore and didn't see a single star for three days.

"Nice lawn furniture." Her smile was playful as the almost sarcastic compliment danced off her lips. She lit a cigarette. Now that Ann doesn't drink anymore, she smokes cigarettes all day long, drinks coffee till two, coke till ten, and tea until she falls asleep. While I'm lying in bed, I picture her bouncing around the confines of her room-- laughing and smoking until the sun comes up.

"Thanks, big purchase of the today, I thought it would add a nice touch--a little spice- to my very nice, and very large, porch."

"At least you don't live with your father anymore."

"Yeah, I only work for him." My eyes were on the sky as we talked. I know the landscape by heart anyway, no need to look any-- where but up. The houses haven't changed in twenty years. The air started whipping at my cheeks, I turned my head into the wind for more. Ann's cigarette smoke found its way over to my nose and then flew out the half-opened window.

"Um...Did you know Mary had her baby...your baby...the baby..." Ann's voice trailed off, and suddenly our usually mindless banter almost slit my throat, cut off all oxygen.

"Well, I knew that...I knew that...I knew that it was almost almost almost almost time for it-her-him-to come out...be born...it's been almost a year...well, I guess nine months, huh?" I laughed nervously as I made an attempt at a joke. My head was shaking back and forth, my eyes twitching in their sockets--a symphony of blinking and blank stares, both knees seemed to have a mind of their own, and tears were pushing their hardest to start flow-ing--I shoved them back. Rolling down the window, my hand moved through the cold air in waves, a few drops of rain began tickling my arm--or trying--it felt more like open safety pins being thrown by little children at my bare skin. The houses blurred into an oblivion of black, the street swept out from under me, the stars nothing special in the sky.

"Listen, Matt, she wrote me a letter, I just opened it today. She sounds good, she doesn't want to talk to you, but she wanted you to know." I knew Ann had more to say, but I cut her off.

"Jesus, I have a little…"

"…girl…Jessica." Ann filled in.

"Girl," I repeated slowly. "Jessica," I repeated even slower.

"Matt, it's going to be hard, but you need to move on—she doesn't want you to see her."

"Can I have her address?" I didn't even really feel like a dad--I felt like I was reading that story in Health class, the one they make you read in sex education, in an attempt to stop sex before marriage, where the adolescent father turns out to be an asshole, leaving the reader wondering why the story isn't turning out right. But I was dead to emotion. My tears stopped pushing at my eyelids, my body silenced. I was a freak. I was a goddamn unfeeling, asshole freak father. Can I have her address? I repeated the question over and over in my mind as Ann silently drove. What kind of question is that? Suddenly I felt my body begin shaking again, but out of anger--pure anger--like I felt when I heard the rednecks in town beat up a black man running down the street--like I remember trying to control when my mother left--an anger you can't understand--an anger that starts slowly and then takes over all you know--the houses, the street, the sky, you hands, your feet. How could Mary do this to me? She's making me a bad father without giving me a chance--she chose my fate for me. Who gave her that power? Who put her in charge of my life?

"We're here." Ann said it as though I'd been waiting for this destination all my life. My lips didn't move--neither did I. "Listen Matt, we need to put the past in the past-things happen. That's why I want you here tonight--these people were almost completely gone-- lost to the world at some point in their lives--even at this point in life. Maybe they'll help, in some twisted searching way." She said the last part with her forehead all wrinkled, her head cocked to one side, not sure of what exactly she was hoping for. Her tiny hand was squeezing my shoulder. "You're not going to be a part of Jessica's life,

Matt...you just can't be." Her hand found the handle of the door, it opened. Ann turned back to me, her feet on the concrete, "Mary is going to finish college--she's very happy--she is actually engaged." Ann said the last part fast--she knew she couldn't keep anything from me--perhaps she thought it would make me feel better, relieved even.

"Why isn't she marrying me?" I asked quietly. But Ann had already shut her door and started toward the big white doors of the building. My hands were insistently tapping the glove compartment--in no rhythm--just in anger. After three attempts at opening the door, I finally got out. Following her, my mind was a jumble of string tied in knots, my stomach an erupting volcano of acid, my lips closed tightly. The train's whistle was blowing in the background, soothingly, I suppose. I knew Ann well enough to know that she didn't mean to break me with her last words, I knew she felt as though she had to pay me back for all the nights I guarded her. Maybe some boys would be glad to not have to deal with a family right now--in a lot of ways I was--but at the same time I felt robbed. The parking lot was almost completely empty--and for some reason it smelled funny, like wet cats or something. On a better night--I knew I would have associated it with winter or falling leaves--not tonight though.

"Do you really want to marry her, Matt? Jesus, come on!" She had stopped so suddenly I almost ran into her. Her words were angry, but soft somehow. Her green eyes were looking straight into mine--solidly. I had to look away. "You didn't even love her-remember? You're fucking this all up in your twisted little over analytical mind, sweetie." The sweetie was biting--patronizing. I couldn't say anything; I just stared at her, her little nose red in the cold night air, her cheeks flushed with earnestness. "Stop fucking with yourself, Matt." With that she turned on her heel, focused on the door, her black hair shining, her shoulders slumped to the ground, her step quick in spite of itself. I followed Ann silently into the gray building; the wet cat smell intensified as the air of the room attacked my nose. I don't know why I didn't start walking home, I guess I knew she was right--although it was too easy to admit--if I admitted she was right, I felt like I would immediately turn into a failure. The door slammed behind me. The fluorescent lights blinded me.

* *   *   *   *

The circle of people inside the building was almost exactly what I had expected--the perfect stereotype of these kinds of sessions. All different addicts represented, coffee and cookies--and a lot of cigarettes. Ann poured herself some black coffee, picked me up a few sugar cookies with smiley faces on them, and led me to a seat--she never met my eye. I looked at the pale, sunken-in faces, fidgety hands lost in oversized sweaters, tired eyes, and hopeful smiles. What did I come for? A story? A look? A feeling of understanding shot across the room? I didn't even know where these people were coming from. I had always pictured these "meetings" after Ann would get home--she never said much about them, just generalized the kinds of addicts, their stories, their dreams. It actually always amused me in some way--I never felt like it was real. But it was. I looked at Ann; her tiny hands rhythmically tucked her short hair behind her ear--maybe twenty times a minute. Her eyes were focused deeply on the ground, as if she expected something to come flying out of the fake marble squares: cake, violets, little birds, playground equipment, sanity, screams, the truth, the end. I didn't know. Maybe she just hated me. The ex-heroin shooter, Chip, dressed in a long sleeved black shirt, stonewashed jeans, with legs that went on forever, was slowly explaining how he lost his feet. His limbs were so long they were all tangled in each other--a web of flesh. He sat in a wheelchair--too much heroin between his toes. Every once in awhile I thought he was going to fall asleep--his eyes rolled back, his head bobbed, his words almost stopped--but somehow he kept going. Most people seemed to be pretending to listen. I think most of them were probably writing out their own monologues in their minds.

For some reason "Chip" didn't sound like a heroin addict to me. But I liked him regardless--he talked with sincerity--with remorse--and with hope. I wished I could take him home. Just to sit with him and talk to him--figure out where it went wrong--how it got better. We'd have coffee, sit on the porch, tell stories about high school, junior high, laugh, cry, hug. He'd tell me about the kids who used to beat him up, his father who did the same to his mother, his first dose. I'd listen; shake my head when the time was right. Then he'd listen while I'd tell him about my mom leaving, the child I'm never going to see, my first trip--which was my last. We'd never talk again after he set the coffee cup down on the porch and wheeled him--self away, but it wouldn't matter.

Kelly the "cokehead" was pretty, slightly overweight, but had a sweet face. She was probably in her forties-- she looked like an ex-cheerleader. She spoke quickly-- listening to her was like riding a roller coaster--her words came out too fast to really process what she was saying. She almost committed suicide without even realizing it. Almost jumped off the thirty-first floor of a Holiday Inn without a second thought. The maid luckily walked in as Kelly climbed to the ledge. I felt like it was a made up story--as if I'd seen it in too many movies to actually believe it happened, but when I looked at her, I knew she was telling the truth. The lines around her eyes told the story within their deep and saddened crevices.

I wondered what the hell Ann was doing there, next to Kelly and that old lady, across from Chip, on a folding card table chair, her hands around a cup of black coffee-- she never had problems like this--why didn't she go to simple AA meetings or something? I would imagine they would be a little easier to handle.

Every couple seconds the names Mary and Jessica would float through my mind--until the names seemed like tangible objects that I could reach out and grab at any moment. I didn't love Mary. But I had to love Jessica, right? Or maybe not. If I never get to know her can I really love her? I didn't know. I didn't get it. A few more, people told their stories as the names took form in my head. I heard bits and pieces--breaking through my confusion and imaginary tangible walls. Jake dealt drugs--all kinds—always--spent what should've been his college years in the "slammer" as he called it. He looked hardened--like he built a wall of stone right behind his pupil right before the back of his head--just stuck it in somehow--maybe through his ears.

Then there was Kathy--your regular run-of-the-mill alcoholic who lost her job and almost her mind. I kept my eyes on Ann mostly; she caught me a few times, her face blank when her eyes met mine. Ronnie still had flashbacks--his eyes danced in his head--he still saw giant butterflies, little green dogs, talking bottles. Most of the time he said he was fine--but he looked too paranoid to really believe that. He didn't look anyone in the eye--just at the white floor, then to the table with the coffee and cookies, to his skinny squirming hands, and then start the cycle again. What a way to exist. He said

most of the time it was the shadows that got to him-- came slithering up to him in broad daylight--in his sleep- less dreamless nights--from out of the roads, and under the water. His life was a nightmare--and he knew it, but he couldn't do anything about it. We were all living in some sort of surreal reality--a dangerous one, where we teetered on the edge of it each morning as we rose, each night as we laid to rest. But we didn't seem to control any of it.

"I wish--I need--the parts to simply add up different- ly," Ann's voice was almost startling, as she began talking with her little voice, turning the long sleeves of her gray sweater into knots as she spoke. "I wish they would mul- tiply--in unanticipated ways. I want to wake up in the morning feeling good for the first time in years--I want to redo it all. Meshing and pulling apart all those moments of my existence to create something brand-new: redo day 12 of year 10, undo day 14. Have more days like 300 of year 22, erase day 1 through 50 of year 21." She looked up for the first time, no tears, but something sad behind her eyes, I looked hard at her tiny face, some sort of intensity- -a power--a strength seemed to be flowing up from the floor to her cheeks. "I want the goddamn calculator that got me here--and I want the person in charge of pushing all the buttons." She was biting hard at her bottom lip as she finished, her gaze still strong. I could hear her inhaling--I could see her chest rising steadily up and down. The room was completely silent for at least two minutes. I felt like I could hear everyone's words scramble--racing one another through their minds--all mimicking mine. All hatched from Ann's desire to go back and start over.

Amen, my dear." Kathy finally said, reaching over to grab Ann's hand. The entire circle seemed to be shaking their heads in unison. Smiles and tears creeping up on their faces.

"That's all for tonight," the "session leader" said. The session leader really didn't seem to do too much except find a time to stop the meeting. Maybe she brought the cookies too. Of course, Ann was the first one to leave the room. She seemed almost embarrassed--or maybe shocked she found the words. I said good-bye to Chip and Kelly, gave a wave to the rest of the circle, not seeming as unified as people started standing up and breaking the curve.

I wandered out to the parking lot just in time to see the back lights of the Volvo pulling away. She left without me. She left me there. But she's the one who brought me here--how could she speed away? I started walking down Mahonning Street, past the same houses, in the back of my mind sure that she would turn around for me.

The air was cool, crisp, perfect, but my body was numb. The road was wet from the light rain, flat, and straight, but my eyes may as well have been closed. My body craved a cigarette, my hands wishing I had the comfort. I needed Ann, and I wouldn't mind having the calculator that got me here either. Delete. Delete it all. That's it. No redo--no repeats--just erase. My feet somehow found their way to Main Street even without my mind. Every time a car went past, which wasn't very often on that country road, my eyes would focus on the road at my feet, my eyes at my shoes, pretending for a second that I couldn't hear the engine approaching--almost didn't turn around, only to turn and stare hard into the window as the car passed. Every second car was familiar--John's parents, Jason Fredrickson's truck, Nancy Burger's Honda, some girl from elementary school's grandmother, each stopped to ask if I needed a ride, each time I said: "No,

just out for a little walk, thanks." Reply: "Okay, Matt, see you tomorrow." When you live in a little town everyone just assumes they're going to see you tomorrow. Hopefully they're right. Someday they won't be. I always thought I would see my mom "tomorrow" and she hasn't been in this town for twelve years. I always thought I would see Mary "tomorrow;" it's been nine months.

When Main Street finally led me to my little shack of a house, I prayed she would be sitting there--like a final scene in a Hallmark commercial, with tea cups and a hug, the last shot of us embracing in the late fall night, street lights illuminating the porch, her black hair glowing, my arms overtaking her.

I heard the porch swing creaking before I heard her voice. "Remember the night I threw all the furniture off that frat guy's porch in college--smashed it all: the green settee, the white, wooden table, the two matching rocking chairs?" She was sitting Indian Style in the swing, her shoulders pulled close to her chin.

My feet carried me right past her, like they couldn't stop; her eyes tried to come with me, straight to the bathroom. With one swoop the painted glass was in my hand. Down the steps, out the door, to the porch. Then without thinking, without analyzing why, without looking or caring, I let the sailboat smash into a hundred little yellow and purple parts. The streetlight shone through them like a Picasso sunrise, rain started to gently glisten the street, my closed eyes turned up to the stars letting the drops fall on my face.

Laughing I turned to look at Ann--she smiled.

They should have gone to Tango

Laurence Ross

The bright lights of the stage splashed across Kate's face, changing her skin from blue to yellow to purple, chameleon-like. Jason thought her mood seemed to change under the different hues: sad, happy, and bewildered. If only it were that easy in real life, he thought. No, instead he was forced to assume the role of a telephone psychic, expected to at least pretend to know what she was thinking. If not, he might end up on her futon come bedtime, a situation that usually took place at least once a week. Still, by the next morning, over a mug of coffee during the scrambling of showering, hairspray and eye shadow, she would forget all about whatever unforgivable wrong he had committed the night before.

It was snowing, flakes fluttering all around in the middle of the forest. Or at least that is what is supposed to look like. Jason watched with his elbow resting on the arm of his seat and his head resting against his knuckles as young women danced across the stage in their white costumes. They were meant to appear to be snowflakes, but Jason thought they looked more like a bunch of big tissues being swept across the stage. The music form the orchestra swelled with quickening violin strokes, resonating trumpet chords and the chiming of bells.

Jason turned his head to look at Kate sitting next to him, completely absorbed in all activity. Her mouth was open just slightly and her hand, which he had been holding, had gone limp. He regretted not sending his friend Paul to accompany her. The Nutcracker was not exciting at age four when his grandmother took him to go see it. (He had cried at the appearance of the Rat King. How could anyone forget when it had been brought up at every Christmas dinner since?) What made him think he would like it at age twenty-four? Paul was always willing to do that kind of thing. Just one month ago, Paul had offered to take Kate pumpkin picking after hearing Jason complain about spending his day off rummaging around in a pumpkin patch, comparing size and shape. After all, Jason is in the landscaping business; he spent every day in the dirt and vines.

Jason didn't necessarily know how to put into words the particular reasons he liked Kate, which was strange considering they had been dating for over eight months. It was just the combination of all the little things: her tiny fingernails, the expression she had on her face when she was thinking real hard (with her left eyebrow bent in an S shape) how she unconsciously scratched his shoulder when they were just holding each other, watching television. Sometimes he would lay awake at night trying to add up all of these things together, see what he ends up with, and find the answer. But he never was very good at math.

Thick strips of hair fell across the rims of her glasses; white glare reflected off the lenses. She always wore her glasses to "events"—any occasion where she wanted appear more intellectual, even though she only needs them for driving. She made him wear glasses too. He hated it. Putting on a show for all the supposed upper class, the social elite that strut around these events their 100% silk ties, their starched pants and their gold cufflinks. Cufflinks. That was probably what Kate had bought him for Christmas. Never mind about practical things like a pair of jeans or a sweater. Maybe he would buy her a lawnmower out of spite. But he knew that he would never go through with something that outlandish. He would end up running out Christmas Eve buying her a stuffed animal and chocolate, the only presents left on the otherwise empty shelves.

The music switched rhythms into an Arabic style and a single female dancer (quite attractive in her outfit) made her way on stage. She twisted and turned her body at unthinkable angles, tapping finger cymbals together like she was pinching notes out of the air. She reminded Jason of the Moroccan restaurant a few of his buddies had taken him to a couple months ago. Kate had been at night class in mathematical theory. The restaurant's main attraction was its group of belly dancers—women that swiveled between the customer's tables, bells jingling from their hips. Kate did want him to culture himself. That is why they were at the stupid ballet in the first place. "It's not stupid, it's culture," she would warn.

"Culture. Right," he has said upon walking into the main lobby of the theater. Tables were set up against the far wall with another huge on standing in the center—folding tables with imitation red velvet draping. Delicately placed on top were Nutcracker wineglasses, Nutcracker tree ornaments, Nutcracker candle pillars—where were the Nutcracker t-shirts?

There was an infant in the row right in front of them, sitting in the lap of her mother. She was not paying attention to the ballet either. She was starring at Jason, baby eyelashes seeming too big for her face. She smiled at Jason, her mouth wide open, and raised her arms in the air. It looked to him like she was saying 'Take me out of here!' Jason widened his eyes and then stuck out his tongue. The baby, thoroughly amused, gave a small yelp and then hid her tiny fists.

"Shhh," the mother hushed, bringing her index finger

to her lips. "Be good Chantell." Chantell! What a name. Jason felt sorry for the little girl, imagining her in kindergarten wishing her name were something simple, normal. Something easy to spell, like Mary, Patty, or Sue.

The mother pulled out a plastic bag filled with Cheerios. Chantell began mushing palmfuls of cereal in her mouth, the crumbs falling onto the black collar of her dress. She held out her fist, offering to share with Jason. He actually was hungry. He hadn't eaten anything since the peanut butter and jelly sandwich he had had at work during lunch.

Kate elbowed him in the rib. "Are you even watching this?" Jason felt like he was receiving a much harsher scolding than the baby. "My favorite part of the play is coming up right now. It's called 'Tea.' It is fabulous." Jason rubbed his side. Kate's elbow was bony and it had hurt. Humiliated in public with a jab to his pride. He could handle it when they were by themselves—sometimes he even thought it was cute—but in the middle of a crowded theater that was simply unnecessary. But then again, who cared what these country club boys thought?

Jason started to drift in and out of consciousness until he caught himself staring down at a large woman. No, large was not the word, he thought. Mammoth, whale-like—that was it—whale-like. Like she had swallowed eight children, the first eight children that happened to pass by. But somehow she was weaving across the stage as if she were light as a feather in her dress, puffed out as big as the hull of an overturned ship. The music crescendoed, booming to a climatic chord and the eight children exploded form her undergarments, traipsing rather chaotically around in zigzags. That was too much. Jason slid out of his seat and went to the bathroom.

They entered through the doors of Le Petite Café, the new French restaurant in the heart of the city that

Kate had been talking about nonstop. Jason made the reservations a week before and though he knew it was out of his price range, he wanted to treat her. Maybe it would make up for something he did or something he no doubt would do in the future.

"Why did we have to park so far away," Kate said, bitter over the five-minute walk from a side street.

"Valet parking is out of control. I don't like the idea of some stranger riding in my car." Jason hoped that would end the conversation. He was not about to spend a fortune on dinner just so Kate could chew him out.

"What, are you worried someone might crash your car?" Kate was not looking at him, but at the little table in the corner with two fat Italian men wedged into chairs that appeared to be too small to support them. "Because your car is worth so much money. Or maybe you're just afraid the valet may steal your empty soda bottle collection right out of the back seat." She crossed her arms and they stood in silence waiting for the hostess to arrive.

Last month, Jason and Kate had gotten into an argument over their friend Molly's gift. Jason had picked up a bottle of wine and a card for the party but when Kate came home she launched into a tirade because he hadn't chosen champagne. She was the type of person that added up her grocery bill as she placed the items in the house. Whenever she went out to dinner with a group of people she was the one to take the bill and divide up everyone's portion according to what they ate. These were the nuances of retired who gamble their pennies away at bingo, not of a young successful accountant.

Jason remembered how those nuances were hidden in their first weeks of dating. Both too scared to show themselves in full light, the dinner conversations revolved around trivial pleasantries: how it was funny the weather man never predicts the forecast correctly, the effect inflation has on toothpaste prices, relaying insignificant comments on the habits of mutual friends, laughing at all they had in common. They both sat awkwardly encumbered by physical attraction until the check came.

The hostess came to escort Jason and Katie to the table. She led them to the back of the restaurant next to a party of four: two couples clearly older than Jason and Katie who had obviously been drinking for quite some time. The men wore business suits; the wives looked like Christmas ornaments. The gaudy women had matching haircuts—badly died blond hair pushed up into a halo around their faces like gold crowning. Jason thought that if he just stuck a hook through their heads and hung them on a tree, no one would know the difference. It was just a matter of finding a tree that was big enough.

As Jason and Katie pulled in their chairs, the hostess placed the leather-bound menus before them. Jason started to work his way through the gold-scripted entrees. Cassolette d'escargots en homage à Monsieur Cleuvunot, Omble chevalier et ses poivrons Anaheim et piquillo rôtis, Foie gras poelé et sa figue aux Roquefort.

"This is fabulous!" Katie said, reading the menu as intent as a monk at the Bible. "See, isn't it nice?" Her face looked bright even in the dim candlelight. She took off her glasses and put them back in her purse. Jason, still starring at the foreign language laid in front of him, wondered why the prices were conveniently absent. Kate reached across the table and placed her hand on top of his; it was warm.

A waitress came over to ask if they wanted wine with dinner. She had a tattoo that poked out from her collar and went around the back of her neck. Jason was intrigued but he couldn't make out the design and wondered where else it lead to on her body. He was shocked that a woman with such a tattoo would be working in such a restaurant. "What kind of wine would you like to drink this evening?" Kate asked, her features soft and flushed from being out in the cold.

"Order what you like," Jason said. Kate and the waitress began to discuss the various bottles on the list but Jason couldn't help but overhear the conversation going on at the table across from them.

"So I said to him," one of the men at the table began. His hands were waving all over the place and his voice was raised well above the subtle bowing of violins. "No, you are a fool! The phrase 'uh-huh' did not originate in the Philadelphia region but from Boston and its surrounding areas. Can you imagine?" The wives gave exasperated gasps while the other man burst out with an obnoxious cackle. They seemed completely oblivious to the fact that half the restaurant was starring.

"What did we end up with?" Jason asked Kate.

"I ordered a bottle of red."

"But I thought you liked white?" She always ordered white wine whenever they went out. Jason was never a drinker of white wine and preferred red but it was never worth getting in an argument about.

"I do," she said "I'm being nice." She squeezed his hand hard.

"What's the occasion?" Jason said, smirking. He knew he was in danger turning her flash of a good mood sour but decided to risk the sarcastic comment anyway.

"Shut up."

At the table across the way, one of the men banged his fist against the table, rattling silver, crystal and china. "Then do you know what I did when I was over there?" Jason figured the man was trying to get the attention of anyone willing to listen. "I met this little old man on a green hat when I was shopping around the bazaar and you know what he told me? He said 'If you are looking for something really invigorating, I have a friend who runs trips.' And you know what it turned out to be? Rock climbing. Not just any rock climbing. Buddhist monk rock climbing." Jason tried to imagine the tall, big-bellied man in a business suit propelling himself down a mountain side. "So that is where I spent the next three days—climbing rocks next to Buddhist monks." The man, finished with his story, took a large sip of his drink.

"Maybe you should try that," Jason said, turning his back to Kate who had closed her menu.

"What, rock climbing? What for?" She was spinning her glass of water in circles by its base. The condensation was staining the white tablecloth gray. "And you couldn't pay me enough money to spend three days with a bunch of Buddhist monks."

"You would never survive," Jason said, playing with the corners of the napkin in his lap. He spotted a waiter carrying a large tray of assorted entrees, and while he couldn't recognize what anything was outside the rice, the steamy aroma still made his stomach churn. "You might fall off a cliff while checking your palm pilot."

Their waitress returned with a bottle of wine and began twisting the bottle opener into the cork, still holding the bottle in the air. The cork squeaked as she pulled and then made a hollow pop as she finally worked it out. The waitress poured a small amount into two wine glasses. After taking a sip, Kate motioned her approval and the waitress filled each glass halfway before dashing back toward the kitchen.

"You wouldn't either," Kate answered. "I am sure that they are not serving steak and potatoes in whatever country your friend over there is gallivanting through. You are always saying that I have no sense of adventure and you won't even go with me to the sushi restaurant on Market Street."

Jason took a sip of his wine and held it in his mouth for a moment before swallowing. It tingled down his throat. He thought of how nice it would be to slide into bed later, drift off beneath the covers and forget about the giant maple tree he had to saw down the next morning. Some rich bastard ordered the job out of season because the branches were blocking his Christmas light carnival from the view of passing cars. That meant for Jason a torturous afternoon with his ought-to-be-retired coworker Mitch, a skinny man with a yellow beard who liked to tell stories that began with, "Did you ever know the guy?"

"Sushi is uncooked food. That is not a fair example." Jason turned around to see what was taking their waitress so long to come back for their order. He spotted her with a dripping pitcher, refilling water glasses at a table of two older women. "What are you ordering?" he asked.

"Probably the Cote de veau aux asperges, fricassee de morilles et ris de veau," she said, lifting open her menu again. .

"Does it have fish in it?"

"No."

"Then I'll have the same thing."

Jason was so hungry he didn't care what came, as long as it was edible. The wine seemed only to make his hunger more intense. On top of that, he did not want to go through the embarrassing process of having Kate decode the menu. Jason thought his lack of French skills would allow Kate to go off on some intellectual power trip resulting in stories of Paris trips and French classes dating back to junior high.

"But then we won't be able to share," Kate said with her lower lip protruding and her forehead wrinkled. She liked reaching her fork across to his plate in the middle of a meal and stealing a bite of whatever looked good. Splitting a meal was like getting two dinners for the price of one. But Jason knew that it meant Kate was going to order two dishes that she wanted.

"Fine. Just so long as it isn't fish."

It was cold outside; the radio said chance of snow. The moon was not visible but the sky was still lit by the yellow glow of the city lights. It was one of those nights when it is hard to tell where the clouds stop and the sky begins. The lamplight reflected in the street as Jason and Kate made their way back to the car.

Kate had her arms crossed. She was cold despite the thick coat. "I told you we shouldn't have parked so far away. We could be standing behind doors in the heat waiting for the valet to bring the car to us. Now I'm going to have icicles in my hair by the time we get there."

"Would you let it go," Jason said stuffing his hands into his pockets. As they walked he listened to the clicking of her heels and watched the cracks in the cement. The slabs of concrete were uneven, pushed up by the roots of the spruce trees along the road. The cars lined up at the curb were parked with one side on the sidewalk, making the other side tilt down toward the street.

"What are you wearing to my mother's house for Christmas?" Kate asked. She flipped the lapel of her coat up around her neck. Kate's mother had invited Jason over for the family's party. He was not looking forward to Christmas Eve, imagining the hours of uncomfortable conversation with her extended family. He'd be show-cased and scrutinized like a painting put up in a gallery by a new artist. "Well, there is a slight blemish on the right cheek. And the hair is a bit too long, but oh that can be touched up a bit. What does he do again? I think the last one was a little better." Despite the fact that he would try, Jason knew at some point he would use the wrong utensil or say something inappropriate.

During the summer, Jason and Kate had gone to her

uncle's beach house overnight. After dinner, Kate's uncle discovered sand on the couch in the living room and went storming around inspecting everyone's feet and clothing. Jason was convicted, found to have sand still clinging to the back of his shirt. "Imagine, finding sand at the beach!" Jason had wanted to yell but instead just brooded in the blasting noise of the Dustbuster. Kate had tried to tell him it wasn't a big deal but her attempts at encouragement were not enough to counterbalance the uncle's condescending glances.

"I don't know. I'll find something-I'll wear this. Are you sure your mother wants me to come? It seems like a family thing. I don't want to intrude." Kate stopped walking.

"Are you kidding me? We have had this conversation three times already. You are going. How do you think it feels to have people ask how the imaginary boyfriend is?"

Jason found it ironic that she had been so cold she complained about the walk to the car but it was no problem to stand there and yell at him. Her breath rose in front of her, the white fading into the light of the street lamp. "Okay, I was just asking. You don't have to get all huffy."

Jason was sorry to leave behind the Christmas Eve ritual he had started to form over the past couple of years. Dinner at Jacob's House of Matzo where he would chit-chat with the waiter over a bowl of matzo ball soup, then onto a Christmas cartoon marathon until he received the wake up call from his parents the next morning, telling him to come over for brunch and presents. A car drove past; its headlights making their shadows stretch and then shrink back down to normal size again. The car turned and its red tail-lights vanished behind the edge of a row house.

"You just need to learn when to ask and when to keep your mouth shut." Kate complained. She started walking again, heels clicking toward the car. She was a little drunk so he let the comment go. They had gone through the whole bottle at dinner.

Up the block, a small group of people in dark clothing were gathered at the front steps of a porch. One guy was sitting next to a girl with her head on his shoulder and there were two other men leaning against the iron railing, cigarettes burning in their hands. Jason had an ominous feeling. It was late and he had not seen anyone walk by since they left the restaurant. "Let's cross the street," he said grabbing her arm and pulling her toward the curb. She stumbled a little bit and then ripped her arm from his hand.

"Get off! The car is this way. I'm not going out of the way. You can cross if you want to." Kate readjusted her coat and continued on but Jason grabbed her arm again.

"This is not the time to be stubborn. Would you just come on?" Jason looked ahead and imagined the eyes of the men sizing him up. Jason wished for once she would just listen to him without a debate. "I do not want any trouble."

"We have just as much of a right to be on this street as they do. Relax. The car is only two blocks away."

The men were all burly-dark coats, big shoulders-Jason guessed manual labor. One of them had a shaved head and the other two wore hats. The girl on the step had on a skirt and high boots. Her hair was long and dark and hung around her face.

The bald one spoke first. "Can you folks spare some change?"

Jason hoped that if he just continued walking, they might just let them alone. He wished he could telepathically warn Kate to do the same.

"We're just passing through," Kate said, not really looking at any one of them in particular. "Sorry." She folded her arms and took a few more steps before the two men on the railing swept in front, blocking the sidewalk. Jason tucked Kate behind one of his shoulders, not knowing what to expect.

"Now now," one of the other men began, "I'm sure folks as dressed-up as you could give a little something." The guy flicked his cigarette into the street and as it hit the ground, it rolled leaving a momentarily glowing trail of red ash. Jason noticed the man kept shifting his weight from one foot to the other and thought it peculiar. He looked across the street, hoping to see someone walking past, looking for any movement that might change the outcome of the situation. An elderly woman out to walk her dog would have done. Most of the windows were black. One flickered with the colored strobe of television light.

The guy who had been sitting pushed himself off the step. "How's about a look inside that pretty little bag of yours, miss?" He was shorter than the other two, but no less intimidating. Jason thought his hands looked large and muscular.

Kate pulled the strap of her purse closer to her elbow and pressed it against her side. "Jason, come on," she said. "We are going to be late."

Jason couldn't believe she was going to try and push her way through. It wasn't that he thought she was necessarily wrong, just that it was not the ideal place to enact her self-righteousness. But before he had time to react, a man's fist landed flush on his jaw. Jason fell backward onto the pavement, landing on his shoulder. The punch stung in the cold air like Jason thought a belly flop off a bridge into the ocean might feel. His mind submerged into the surreal murky state between alcohol and getting the shit knocked out of you.

The last time he was in a fight was high school, in a park at night, a place where a lot of kids hung out and drank on the weekend. He was there with a few of his friends for lack of something better to do. One of the guys from the basketball team stumbled around as usual. His name was Ray Deamer. He approached Jason for no reason and socked him in the eye. Ray had been holding a roll of quarters in his hand and Jason's eye had swollen shut. Jason's friends told him afterwards that Ray had thought he was somebody else. That old case of mistaken identity--one minute you are walking into the 7-Eleven for a pack of cigarettes and the next you are caged in the back seat of a wailing police car, fingered for rape and headed to the electric chair because you resemble some violent nut. When Jason finally got home, he had to make up some clever explanation about his eye to tell his mother. He and his friends were just wrestling; they were playing baseball in the dark and one of the pitches 'flew too high; he was at the movies and all of a sudden, a super-sized soda landed in his face. For months after, Jason thought of ways to get back at Ray who never even apologized.

Jason was still on the ground trying to figure out where Kate had gone. The bald guy was standing over him, rubbing his knuckles. The next thing Jason knew, the girl in the miniskirt and boots had jumped on the bald one's back like a child might jump on her father's for a piggyback ride. She wrapped her boots around her boyfriend's waist. "Theo, come on baby, let's get out of here. I wanna go home." Her arms looked as if they were practically strangling his neck. Jason noticed for the first time that she had a nose ring. It sparkled in the headlights of a car that was coming around the corner.

"Let's get out of here," he heard one of the guys

repeat, though he could not tell which one.

He listened to the footsteps of the four of them echo down the block till they drifted out of range. The headlights of the car swept over Jason as he was pushing himself off of the ground. The car slowed just a little and then bumped through the next intersection, leaving only its trail of white exhaust. When Jason finally stood up, he found Kate to be in nearly the same spot she had been before he went down, just standing there. For the first time, Jason thought Kate looked scared. "I told you not to park so far away! God, why couldn't you just do something?" she screamed as her eyes welled with tears.

"What were you thinking?" Jason yelled back at her. "Why couldn't you just give them your wallet?" His jaw ached. His shoulder was stiff and it hurt to lift his arm. Jason wondered if she was planning on going to the car. He knew he would be staying at Paul's apartment that night. Kate held the strap of her purse in her hand. Her face was red and blotchy. Jason looked, at her waiting for a response but she remained motionless, her eyebrow bent and her arms down at her sides.

He started walking toward the car, only a couple more blocks up the street. He put his hands back in his pockets and listened for her footsteps to follow. Jason stared down at the sidewalk, tracing along the cracks of the broken pavement with his eyes and trying his best to step around them.

The Spin Cycle
Aileen DePeter

I know the sounds of my Laundromat. I know how each of the two rows of fourteen washers rumble like an eighteen wheeler passing by on a highway. I know how the one wall of twenty-eight dryers sound like voices in another room, echoing faintly. Her washer was fuming, absolutely shaking out of its space. I could see the side of her face. Brown eyes, I think, maybe green? Brown curls, and a crinkled look of concern that half hid them.

"You probably overloaded." I had moved up behind her, she didn't hear me. I cleared my throat. "You probably overloaded." She turned. I could see her whole face now. Brown eyes. They looked at me with surprise. "That's why it's shaking like that. I can help."

"Do you work here?" Her thumb and forefinger of her right hand brushed against the fingers on her left. They stopped and twisted a thin silver ring. She rotated the ring for one final spin. She looked nervous. A small piece of hair fell into her eyes. She swept it back and tucked it behind her ears. She had beautiful hands.

"I, well, I mean I do work here. It's family owned." I was unable to admit my immediate attachment to this place. Truth is, I grew up here sweeping the floors on Sundays for my mother. I would gather up all the little gray-green scraps of lint that littered the floor. I would never be able to make her understand. I remember opening each dryer along the row looking for errant socks and pocket change. Once I found a five-dollar bill tangled in the lint. I was the treasure hunter, each dryer, each washing machine was my own adventure. I had painted the walls here during high school. I wrote my name in big letters across the wall, then slowly filled in the spaces around it with pale yellow paint. The paint was now faded and peeling away where the wall met the floor and the ceiling.

"Oh, I'm really sorry, my washer broke at home and . . . Did I break anything?" She spoke fast; I could see the color in her cheeks.

"Don't worry, it happens all the time." It did, really about once a month somebody would come in unsorted and put two loads worth of laundry into one machine. My roommate in college always had me do his laundry. "Jake, you're like a woman," he would say, "whites in one pile, colors in the other. Don't mix your brights with your whites." My mother had taught it all to me. At stages in my childhood, she would just take me over to a machine and I would just watch her. She always distrusted the dryers at school and would frequently end our phone conversations by telling me to check my clothes every fifteen minutes. I always had sweaters hanging in the window, because it was better to take them out damp and hang them then have them shrink away. She always use to send packages that contained a Laundromat sample size of fabric softener. My roommate and I however, were always the best-dressed guys on the floor.

The washing machine was still shaking. She was back to spinning her ring. The clothes she was wearing were professional looking, but somewhat casual. The jacket to the blue skirt hung over a laundry basket. The white blouse fit her form; her sleeves were rolled up to her elbows. I lifted the lid of the washer and the spin cycle stopped. The room, although crowded with other people, seemed so quiet. I realized that I had been yelling to be heard.

"You can just put half in the other washer, and put it back on the spin cycle." I had gotten half way back to the sanctuary of my counter when she spoke.

"Thanks, I really appreciate it."

In an awkward move, I twisted backwards, while trying to go forwards. I felt gawky and absurd. She laughed a little, but it wasn't a mocking laugh. When I finally got my gaze back to hers, feet forward, face back, my cheeks felt warm.

"No problem, anytime." I answered

"I have a great recipe for vegetarian lasagna." She was standing at my counter. Her hands tapped on the counter top, a silver necklace fell beneath the collar of her shirt. She hunched over, her smooth elbows just hanging over the edge of the counter. She was smiling. I didn't say anything. This was the fourth time in three weeks that she had been here. I felt as if we had an understanding of embarrassment between us. Hers was for the overload, mine for the awkwardness of my own self.

"I once took some cooking classes." It sounded loud, and for a moment, I wondered if I had even spoken, or if I was still trying to comprehend what she said.

"Well then I guess it's settled." Her hair was up today, pulled back in a little knot at the base of her head. There were these little wisps of stray hair highlighted in the "Wash and Dry" neon light in the window.

"Settled?" I wondered what it would be like to undo the knot in the back of her hair and watch as it falls down over her shoulders.

"Dinner, vegetarian lasagna, your place?"

I tipped the chair back to the white cement wall, leaned my face toward the small plastic fan, and closed my eyes. I could hear the whirl of the fan at my ears and the scratch of an errant zipper scraping the inside of a dryer. We never made vegetarian lasagna in my cooking class.

"I guess, I mean, dinner sounds all right, it sounds good." My voice in its nervousness seemed to deepen, and I found myself speaking in a low monotone voice. I cleared my throat.

"Yeah, good." I repeated. She told me her name was Donna. The first day we met, the day the washer overloaded, I watched her wrestle with coils of wet clothes with those beautiful hands.

The last date I was on was in college. We went to dinner and a movie. Her name was Kathy or Katie; she laughed too loud and had long blond hair that reached the seat when she sat down. She ordered a strawberry milkshake. I could still taste it on her when I kissed her. I never anticipated anything from those college relationships. It was always more physical than anything else. I even dated one girl for a whole year. We would talk about the future. I liked the way she smelled. She never made me wonder why she was like the way she was. I never questioned why she might be interested in me. I just knew she smelled good, and she was willing to be there. My mother didn't like her and always called her by the wrong name, Lisa instead of Linda. Once she came down for a week over Christmas break. She left two days early because my mother had a habit of talking about her, while at the same time pretending she wasn't in the room.

Donna said that she would bring the groceries, all I had to provide was the dinner table and a bottle of wine. I stared at the China plates that I had been left by my mother after she died a year ago. I didn't really lie to Donna when I said the Laundromat was family owned. It was, by my mother for twenty-six years. It was now my sole property with her Queen Anne China plates, Ginger her dog, and her collection of Lawrence Welk records. The records I couldn't stand, but I couldn't stand to get rid of them either. They still smelt like her- musty and stained with perfumed oily hands. It was the one way I could hear her memory.

"Ginger, go lie down!" She was trailing after me getting underfoot at every turn. His brown coat brushed up against my pant leg, leaving fine brown hair behind.

"Come on, girl, this is important, you'll see." I bent down to pet her. "You know, I just washed these pants." She seemed to understand, either from the sound of my voice or the pained look I probably had on my face. She limped off and lay down on her doggie bed. My mother had insisted on getting a dog after I left for college. She thought that she would need some protection. Ginger is anything but an attack dog. She was a chocolate lab and had been hit by a car. She had a limp, hardly ever barked, and was content just to lie around. Still, she gave my mother the same company she gives me now. Every Sunday my mother used to call me at school. She insisted that I say hello to the dog. Those conversations always focused on if I was studying enough, sleeping enough, and doing my laundry. I never really asked about her. In fact I half listened most of the time when she said anything.

I took out two china plates and two of my mother's Waterford crystal wineglasses. I guess I was lucky, most guys my age don't have china patterns and the Colleen collection of Waterford crystal glasses. The whole house had the same furniture as when I grew up. All the stuff I brought back from my apartment at school was sitting in the basement. I hadn't even bothered to bring them in. I did take the plastic off the couch cushions though. The plastic was cracked and yellowed, but the fabric on the sofa looked brand new. I wondered if my mother ever knew that. She had photographs on the shelf of her corner cabinet. There was one of me in third grade, and a picture of her and Ginger. There were none of the two of us together. I took the good silverware out of the drawer beneath the pictures. I could hear my mother's voice.

"Forks on the left, Jake, forks on the left." The table was ready.

"Jake, do you cry when chopping onions?" She had just walked in the door. Already her hands were in the bag starting to unpack. She was wearing a simple yellow sundress. 100% cotton, I thought. Her hair was down.

"No, I mean, it doesn't really bother me," I said.

"Good because it makes my eyes so teary. I'll start the water for the lasagna." She pulled out the box of lasagna from the bag.

"The pots are under the stove." I said, peeling back the first layer of the onion skin. I watched her rifle through an array of pots until she found the right one.

"I know that you were a master chef in your cooking classes, but I hope store bought pasta is okay."

"You mean it's not hand pressed?" I felt a little bolder in her presence.

"I can make that for you if you wait about six years, but I'm hungry now." She opened the box, sliding her fingernail beneath that cardboard line and in one clean line, opened it.

"You have a nice place here. I like your plants." She put the box back on the counter and looked around. I had bought the plants that afternoon, in an attempt to make this place seem less stifling, for both Donna and myself. I noticed that one of the plants still had the price tag on its silver foil wrapping. They did, however, brighten the room a bit. With the exception of the five years I was away, I had always lived in this house. My time seemed divided between it and the Laundromat. The house always shrouded in a tint of gray; the Laundromat with its yellow walls and fluorescent lights was always a brighter place.

The smell of sautéing onions quickly overtook the room. I had forgotten how much I enjoyed cooking. It seems I haven't eaten for the past two years. When my mother was ill, I would make myself a sandwich or order a pizza. I would cook only out of necessity, never out of desire. After she died, I found it was easier to go out and eat. Three times a week for the past year I have been occupying a counter seat at Jimmy's Oasis Grill on the corner of Main and Third Ave. I have become a regular.

"You live here all alone right? What is it, three bedrooms?" Donna took the long line of pasta and dropped it easily into the salted boiling water.

"Oh I don't live alone, I have Ginger and the plants."

She laughed, and for a moment I thought she was content with that for an answer. There was a small pause. I stirred the onions. She was waiting for an explanation. Her mouth was slightly open and her head tilted to the side. She looked as if she was going to say something, but stopped.

"This was my mother's house, she died about a year ago. The Laundromat was hers too; I inherited it, along with Ginger. The plants are mine."

"I'm sorry." She blushed a little and poked at the pasta. "I always ask the wrong questions."

I shrugged. "Don't worry about it, it happens all the time." Actually it didn't. I wasn't used to explaining my life to anyone else. The words felt odd coming from my mouth. I had always rehearsed what I would say if placed in the situation. At nights sometimes I would say to myself, "My mother's dead, this is her stuff, her life, I am just here because I have no place else to go." Donna looked up from cutting tomatoes.

"That is the same line you used in the Laundromat, 'It happens all the time.'"

"That really does happen, a lot of people overload, maybe not all the time, but some people feel its necessary to put three or four hundred pounds of in one machine." I got her laughing and my own awkwardness of having to admit my position, laundryman, inheritor of an older generation, carrier of the weight, faded.

"Ginger's a beautiful dog." She was right; I had never really looked at her, always past her. "Look at the way the light hits her. You should really keep those blinds open, you have great light." She smiled at me then turned away and drained the pasta into the sink. Ginger's coat shone in the late day sun coming the window. I had finally cleaned the windows, aware of wiping away so much more.

I watched her eat, and she caught me staring too many times. She would smile and look down at her plate, her brown hair falling in front of her eyes. I wonder if she talks to her mother. They probably have one of those relationships where they call each other every week, maybe more than once. Did she tell her mother she met a nice guy at the Laundromat? Her mother probably asked what I did for a living. She would have to tell her I worked there; I wasn't doing my laundry there. Did she twist the ring on her finger when she spoke on the phone? I hope she didn't feel bad for me. In third grade I found a frog on the sidewalk on my way home from school. I had pitied it, saw it was helpless. I brought it to the Laundromat and put it in a washing machine. I thought it needed water.

"So you went to college to become a chef?" One side of her mouth curled up into a small smirk.

"The dinner is that bad?" I asked. She was fully smiling now. She had very straight teeth.

"No, really it is very good. I was just wondering."

"Actually, I was a business major. I took cooking classes as electives. They really helped out in my gopher job at the insurance firm I worked at before I had to come back here. I could make the best cup of coffee in the whole office."

"Did you like it?" She seemed interested, but I kept wondering why she would want to be here with me now.

"It was okay, I don't think I really had any idea of what I wanted to do, or be, so the job to me was fine. I guess it was no different from anything else." It was true, if I hadn't worked there I could have done the same job at any number of places. I was one of the masses, the average worker, doing the average job. I lived in a small apartment, met my friends who hadn't moved on, on weekends, and went to work. I had always thought that eventually I would rise above the messenger boy role, and be able to become my own boss. I just didn't think it would be the boss of a Laundromat.

"Your job now seems better then that. You own your own business, and you seem to know a lot about it."

"How much is there to know?" I had always tried to think of a way to put 'I watch people do laundry all day' on a resume. I picked at the last pieces vegetable lasagna that stuck to Queen Anne China pattern on my plate. I was suddenly terrified that there might be spinach on my teeth.

"You knew how to fix my run-away washing machine." She poured herself a glass of wine and leaned back in her chair. "You know, I didn't even know you were behind me that day. I was so caught up in what I did wrong, and how

I was going to fix this out of control washing machine that I didn't even hear you talking to me. You just reached over and all the noise stopped. I thought, why didn't I do that? It was so simple." She was looking directly at me.

"I grew up in that place, it was my babysitter. I know by heart which dryer takes the longest to dry and which one will shrink your favorite shirt if you put it on for an extra fifteen minutes. I don't even think about it really." I realized my voice had become harder. "Ever since I can remember I did odd jobs that place. I used to watch the regular customers coming in at the same time on the same day, every week. There was one lady, Mrs. Jackson, who wore the same sweat suit every time she washed her clothes. For five years I saw her in nothing but a pink and gray sweat suit." Ginger brushed up against my leg under the table. I handed her a piece of Italian bread. She licked the ends of my fingertips in gratitude. "Sunday afternoons were the busiest days. In the summer the heat was so unbearable until we got air conditioning I used to run around in just a pair of shorts. My mother would dress nicely every day. She would greet the customers with a smile, like they were the most important people in the world. I would be running along the aisles, barefoot, with a dirty face." I looked up to see if she was still there. There were all these memories that I suddenly found myself wanting to tell her.

"You know, Jake, you're lucky you have such a connection to where you work. You could still be a gopher making coffee."

"But it would be the best coffee." She laughed. "I could also be a fabulous curator of the Art Gallery. Downtown's finest."

"Let's not forget that it is downtown's only art gallery. I see the subject has changed to me." She smiled and moved her chair in closer to the table. "You know I love working there, but I sometimes still wish I was holed up in some studio apartment turning out clay pots and modem paintings." I watched as her hands moved when she talked. They were in harmony with her words. I knew she had creative hands.

"Once I made a pinch pot and glazed it dark blue. My mother put it on the counter of the Laundromat, but she never put anything in it."

"Well, not all pinch pots have to be functional." She picked up the plate from the table and I followed her back into the kitchen.

"I've never been to the art gallery." I remember passing it one day and wondering why it was just called the Art Gallery and not anything else.

"I'd never been to the Laundromat before my machine broke. So now we're even."

I didn't really believe that.

Donna hummed when she dried dishes, little made up songs in her head. The only hum I knew was the rumble of the washing machine.

"So what kind of art do you have at your gallery?" I handed her the last dish and turned off the faucet. She dried the plate and her hands with the same towel, then handed it to me.

"Mostly modern paintings, photography, some sculpture. Nothing like what you
would see in Europe."

"You've been there?" Now she was a world traveler. All I knew of the outside world was Bermuda shorts and French cut jeans.

"A few times. I love Italy, Florence especially. I felt so unknown there, but it was like I was still a part of all the history around me. I don't know how much sense that makes. I have always wanted to be important, not fame or wealth, but important in what I did, important to other people. I just feel so, I don't know what the word is…"

"Anonymous." I said it because I knew that is what she meant. I knew what it felt like to be anonymous and I wondered what it was Donna wanted.

"Right. I guess everybody needs a history. When I was surrounded by so much of it, I felt like I had my own history too. I wasn't just some American tourist taking pictures. I felt an attachment to something better. It was beautiful there. I would love to go back." She shrugged and tossed her hair behind her shoulders with one quick flick of the wrist. "Have you ever been?"

"No never. My mother went once, a few years before I left for college. It was one of those special deals, she went with the church. I think all they saw were European churches—she has hundreds of pictures of them that she kept in an album."

"It must be very hard to live in her house, with all that stuff."

I found myself shuffling a bit on the floor, almost swaying in an attempt to defray the question. My mother and I had never been close. Once when I was fourteen I found her looking through my room. She just turned to me and told me everything I had she had given to me, and that she has as much right to my stuff as I did. I said nothing. And that silence hung in the air sunk into the corners and started to stifle me. I remember feeling bad for her but never knowing what it was she needed in order to feel better. I saw her one morning as I stood on top of the stairs and watched her cry, consoling herself that it wasn't her fault that my father wouldn't be coming home. I let her life melt into mine and now the edges are all blurred. Mail still comes addressed to her, and courtesy calls because she was always a good consumer. I have her job, her home, her china pattern.

"Yeah, I guess it is."

I knew that I would be sleeping alone that night, with the exception of Ginger at my feet. I couldn't ask Donna to try to become a part of my life, when I wasn't even sure whom or what I wanted anymore. The door closed behind her and I watched form the window as she got into her car. The street light gave just enough glow that I could see the outline of her face as she turned on the radio and pulled away.

It was raining the next day. I had been sitting in the Laundromat waiting for the people to come in. My mother used to say that nobody liked to do laundry in the rain. The hot summer days, the humid ones; those were the days when everybody came out. Those were the days that people stuck to the glossy pages of magazines waiting for the spin cycle to end. They folded newly bleached clothes with ink stained hands from doing newspaper crosswords. The only person who had come in so far today asked to post an advertisement on the front of my counter. I had told him to go ahead. The flyers hanging there were ragged with wear, and the tape had lost its stickiness from the combination of the hot dryer air mixed with the coolness of the air conditioning. People put out hope on

these photocopied pages with tear off numbers frayed like the edge of the pillow. I am always surprised to see one missing.

"Morning, Jake." The door had opened with the ring of the bells.

"Morning, Eddie." He nodded as he dragged in a wet sack of laundry the door. Eddie always did his laundry on Friday mornings. Technically he was my tenant. He lived in the apartment above the Laundromat. He and my mother had long since reached an agreement: all Eddie paid for was laundry. I didn't mind it. Eddie had been around long before I had. He was always full of stories about my childhood. His favorite was to tell how I fell off the ladder he had put up to his apartment window when he was repainting the outside of the Laundromat. Apparently, I thought I could fly. Good thing I had only gone up a couple of rungs, good thing I was, at that point, afraid of heights.

"Jake, I got something for you." He put his hand into a satchel that hung across his chest and hit his hip as he walked. "I've been meaning to give this to you. I just keep forgetting." Eddie was a small man, not taller then five four. I never could remember him with hair, although at some point he must have had some. The fluorescent lights that reflected off the top of his head gave him the halo look of an angel. "Your mother gave this to me once to borrow, and I never gave it back to her. I just found it when I was looking under my bed to see if I dropped any laundry." He pulled out an old Swiss Army Knife. "I think I used it to unpack some boxes once, I guess I just forgot to return it." He laid the knife down on the counter.

"You can keep this, Eddie." I didn't know what I was going to do with a pocketknife, and there was so much of my mother's stuff that I had never gone through, I didn't need to add to it.

"No, no, I couldn't. It's yours." He smiled and dragged his load of laundry over to washer number three. Eddie never separated his clothes, which was okay because he mostly wore a rainbow of grey. I flipped the knife through my fingers like I would a pen or how my friends in school used to tip back in their chair with a quarter flipped from thumb to pinky and back again. The red surface was cool and smooth. By mid-afternoon, I had carved my name into the back of the counter, inch deep. I traced the edges with my fingertips, stared at my name, and wondered where it came from.

There were two messages on my machine when I got home from work that day. One was from Donna inviting me to the Art Gallery for a photography exhibit. The other was from a catalog company looking for my mother.

"Ginger, come here girl." I knew she would be sleeping somewhere in the grey of this house and refuse to come. I climbed the stairs in search of her. Sprawled on my mother's bed, she lifted her head in recognition, then let it fall onto the quilted bedspread. Everyday since my mother's death I have felt a little more stifled and suffocated by her past and her memories all holed up in this house. I had taken all her clothes and medical equipment out of the room. Everything else was essentially the same. The room was just a bed, the dresser, and a small recliner chair. Her smell was almost tangible, I had tried to mask it with sautéing onions, and vegetable lasagna, but it permeated. There were sealed boxes under her bed, boxes I never really took the time to look into. I pulled them out, Ginger whimpered from the bed above, I sliced them open with the cool red knife from my pants pocket.

Donna told me when she was small her mother used to dress her up when she had parties. Then her mother would tell her to sit very quietly in the corner and not to disturb her unless it was very important. She told me she used to imagine herself inside the paintings on the wall. It was her only way out. God, I liked the way she said my name.

I cut through the third box. It contained boxes within boxes of photographs. There was a photo of my mother standing in front of the Laundromat. It was the first day it opened. A large red ribbon hung on the door. I hardly recognized her. She was old and frail when I knew her, not young and smiling. I could count six washers through the window. It would be two more years until I entered that picture. There were three boxes devoted to me only, from my first to my fifteenth birthday. Everything was categorized by year. My mother had written in her large curvy manner, Jake: 1-5 years, Jake: 6-10 years, Jake: 11-15 years. My whole life laid out before me, memories I couldn't remember, places I thought I had never been. Here was my history. My favorite picture came out of a box marked Jake: 6-10 years. I was sitting on the same white counter I had carved my name in, in front of a tower of clean towels, holding a lollipop. I had no responsibility, I was in the Laundromat, and my mother had given me a treat. That day I slid on my knees on .the newly waxed floors of the Laundromat. I was invincible. Beneath those boxes was my mother's album of her trip to the European Churches. She was standing in front of an indistinguishable church, the light from the stained glass outlining her entire body. She was not smiling, rather, she had a look of understanding, acceptance, that her life was not what it was supposed to be.

I found their letters, love letters, written before they got married. My father had small neat handwriting. He went over his letters twice with a pencil. His words were dark and you could see how they pressed into the piece of paper behind it. My mother had the same curvy line of writing, that was on the boxes that bore my name. The letters were wrapped up in a blue ribbon and tucked in bottom of a shoe box marked: Before Jake. I wondered as I often did when as a child, if I was the reason they fell apart. My father always seemed so large to me. He smelt of aftershave lotion, even though his beard always felt stubbly. I can remember feeling so small as he picked me up in his large, rough hands. My mother recognized him in me. I used to hear her mumbling that I was like my father.

The light in the room started to fade, I was getting

hungry. Ginger had left the room an hour earlier and was probably panting by the front door to go out. I slid the photo of my stained-glass mother out of the plastic casing that she stood behind and put her in an empty frame on the dresser of her room. I packed everything back up tight and pushed it all back under the bed. I had seen it, my life catalogued and remembered.

"Ginger, let's go." I called down to her and she let out a little yelp. The rain had subsided into a light mist. I locked the door behind us.

It was hot out. The Laundromat was packed with people. I had installed two large fans at each end of the room. They just blew hot air back and forth. A small boy took his shirt off and leaned against the cool metal of a washing machine. He was trying to escape the heat. He reminded me of myself. If I closed my eyes, I could still see my mother sitting behind the counter watching what went on around her. I knew that I never really got to know her. I did the things I thought she would want me to do. I never really asked what those things were. I remember her looking over at me, and I was afraid that she was going to yell at me, because I had left my shirt on the floor. She just smiled. Did she ever know I loved her? I had taken care of her, and resented her for that, for making me live her life. All I ever wanted to do was to be let in, not left over to make sense of everything after she left. I traced the outline of my name with the tip of finger. I wish I understood her before I inherited her life.

"Jake?" It was Donna. I hadn't even heard the ring of the bell on the door. The machines were all making a low droning sound.

"I have something for you. I made you a pinch pot." She handed me a

blue piece of pottery. "You can keep it on the counter. You can put penny's in it, or paper clips." I didn't say anything, I just kept looking at her. "Jake?" She waved her hand in front of my face. "Are you okay?"

I rotated the pinch pot in my hand. It was asymmetrical. Donna had carved her initials in the bottom. I wondered why the bottom of pottery isn't glazed. Donna took the pot from my hand and placed it on the counter.

"I dropped the other one."

"What?"

"I dropped it. The one I made, it broke into three pieces, I tried to glue it. It slid off the counter right here." I traced the edge of the counter top with my hand. A dryer buzzed in the background, the kid with no shirt hopped on top of a machine as it went into the spin cycle.

"What is this about Jake?" She ran her fingers through her hair and started to sway slightly back and forth.

"My whole life was catalogued under my mother's bed. I think she left it there for me to find. Everything, second grade report cards, a macaroni necklace I made in pre-school, my acceptance letter to college, everything." The kid on the washing machine was laughing. "Not everything I do falls apart." I wondered if she heard me. She was twisting her ring with her finger.

"Do you even know why I made this for you? I wanted to do something simple, something you would appreciate, something from me. You are so wrapped up in feeling like you are living your mother's life, you don't even realize that other people need you. I need you." She was whispering now. Her voice was getting lost in the sounds of t-shirts and sweat socks hitting the sides of dryers.

"She catalogued my life, she didn't let me live it." The little boy was kicking his feet against the side of the washer. His mother was scolding him from the wall of dryers.

"You don't let yourself live it Jake."

"What am I supposed to do? Look around, all I have is this place. The Laundromat is mine. The rows of washers, the rows of dryers. They are the constant hum that makes me remember; I am the laundry man, the guy who moved back in with his mother. I still sleep in the same small bed I had in high school."

"What are you supposed to do? Do what you want Jake, nobody is forcing you into this life. It seems as if you revel in your misery. And what is that, all you have is this place? Thanks a lot. You have me, and I want you in my life." She was staring directly at me. I had never seen her so angry. I looked away first because I knew she was right.

"Jake, here is the ladder, now remember, no flying." Eddie laughed as he brought the ladder through the door to the Laundromat.

"No flying?" Donna looked up from the paint can she was stirring. Her hands were speckled with yellow spots. Her hair was back, and one small piece kept falling in front of her eyes. I watched her brush it back with the back of her hand, only to have it fall again.

"Don't ask." I smiled at her.

"What, Jake never told you the story of how he could fly?" Eddie's bald head shook back and forth in mock disbelief. I heard him telling her the story as I climbed the ladder and scraped off the last layer of old yellow paint. Donna was laughing, and Eddie was almost doubled over on the floor.

"You should have seen him, you should have seen him." Eddie was barely able to get the words out. Donna was going to paint a mural on one wall. She had it all drawn out and numbered on the wall. I wondered if this was how they painted stained-glass churches.

"He was only on the third rung?" Donna asked Eddie, he just nodded laughing.

"It was the fourth rung." I called over to them. I had hung one of Donna's paintings behind my counter.

"And you thought you could fly?" She looked up at me.

"I knew I could," I whispered to myself. "Yeah, yeah, I did." I told her.

She still hadn't gotten her washer fixed. We do our laundry here together. Eddie walked out of the Laundromat still laughing.

"I'll come down for that ladder later Jake." He called out beneath the ring of the bells on the door.

"Here you go." Donna walked towards me and handed me a can of blue paint.

I would start painting the sky. In the top left hand corner where the row of dryers meets the wall, I wrote my name in big blue letters. Underneath I wrote Donna's and then I filled in the spaces in between.

Twelve Steps

Karen Laird

Step 1

Lexie, my roommate, walks downstairs at three in the afternoon, wearing nothing but a turquoise bra and matching floral underwear. Her disheveled black hair covers the upper half of her slight, boyish frame. She is tiny, only ninety-two pounds, which makes her protruding round beer belly especially conspicuous when partially naked. I am, once again, doing the dishes, trying to ignore her forced sighs as she searches frantically for matches. She asks me groggily, "What are you doing up so early?" She walks into the bright, yellow kitchen, faces me with her left hand resting on the black laced elastic of her panties, her right hand pushing wisps of hair off her forehead. "I mean, what time did you get in last night?" She feigns confusion.

I carefully set down my sponge and place an ivory china tea cup overturned on the drying rack. "Lexie, I picked you up from work, don't you remember?" Of course she doesn't remember. I don't know why I still go along with this routine.

"Oh, gosh, I'm so sorry. I guess I remember that my car wouldn't start. Did I call you?" She prances over to the refrigerator and flings open the door, causing a magnet and the two postcards it was holding up to fall to the linoleum. "Damn it." She kicks them aside with her bare feet. "Did someone drink all my soda?"

"I don't know, I just got back. This morning was my day to work at the shelter. I told Sister Helen that I'd pick up the bread and cheese for tomorrow, so I can get you more soda when I go shopping."

"Don't worry about it." She is drinking my orange juice instead, straight from the carton. "Did I call Scott last night, or did I just have a nightmare?" She giggles and lights her cigarette off the stove.

I take an exaggerated deep breath. "Lexie, you woke him up at three a.m. again. His girlfriend got on the phone and bitched me out when I pulled the receiver from you. You can't keep doing this. He's going to think you're psycho."

"Oh, God, what did I say? Is he mad at me? Maybe I should call and apologize." She checks the clock and rushes towards the phone.

"I really don't think it would do any good." Should I tell her she made a complete ass of herself, or let her wonder? I turn off the burner for her. "Do you have to work tonight?"

"No, Megan picked up my shift." She sits down at the kitchen table, pushing aside the piles of Washington Posts and Baltimore Suns. "Do you really think I have a problem?"

I sit down across from her and begin separating the recent editions from last week's. That familiar cue- I know my next lines by heart. "I told you, Lexie, you pick a program. I'll go with you, anywhere you want. I really think it's time you do something."

"You're right. I know you're right. I'll think about it."

Step 2

I grab my coat and gloves from the closet. "I'm

going to the store now. Do you need anything?" Lexie is wrapped up in a blanket now, flipping through soap operas on the only three channels we get.

"Yeah, actually, would you mind picking up a bottle of wine? Beringer, or something kind of nice? I was thinking of making us dinner. That would go nice with grilled chicken, don't you think?" She rummages through the contents her backpack, which lies on the coffee table. "Could you get me a pack of cigarettes, too? I thought I had a whole pack, I guess I lost them last night." She overturns her bag, spilling change, lipstick, a compact, and tampons onto the sofa. "I can't find my wallet, either. Shit. Can you spot me and I'll get you back?"

"Sure, Lex." I mentally add ten more dollars to the ever-increasing bar tabs that I've covered for her. Whenever Lexie has any money, she spends it on other people. "No problem."

Step 3

An hour later, she has put on a white tee shirt. She is attempting to straighten up living room, and is singing along with Mick Jagger on the stereo. "Carrie, I have to show you the most hysterical thing." She walks over to the stereo and jerks the needle off the record. She picks up the scratched Rolling Stones *Rewind* and tosses it onto the hardwood floor. "Look what my mom sent me." She laughs and hands me a pink Hallmark card.

I open it up to see a biblical verse written out in her mother's neat, cursive hand: "Flee the evil desires of youth, and pursue righteousness, faith, love and peace, along with those who call on the Lord out of a pure heart. 2Tim 2:22" I called Lexie's mother last Friday night frantic when she crashed her 1976 Ford hatchback into the neighbor's Volvo. I explained to her for the third, since I'd moved in with Lexie that her daughter has a severe problem. She thanked me for being such a concerned friend, and left me with these words of wisdom: "Carrie, all we can really do is pray for Alexis. Jesus will help her find right path." I believe in God as much as the next person, but Jesus isn't going to foot the bill for the McHughs' dented fender.

"Isn't that the gayest thing you've ever seen?" Lexie smirks as she pulls a Beatles album out of a tattered jacket. "God damn holy rollers! Now you see why I can't handle going home? Ugh, I need a cigarette." She searches through two brown paper bags that I've set down on the table. I walk into the kitchen grab two wine glasses, knowing that there is nothing I can say to smooth over of the anger she has for her father, or the resentment she has for her mother for staying with him. By the time I return, she is already drinking from the bottle. Guess I should know by now to buy my own.

Step 4

I'm sautéing the chicken and carrots while Lexie takes a shower. I hear the bathroom door open, and she yells cheerfully down the stairs, "Wow! That smells delicious." I make the salad, set the dining room table, and sit down to wait for the chicken. I look around the room, which is my favorite in our house. The table was my family's old kitchen one, and my mom donated it when they remodeled. The roses that Lexie's manager surprised her with for Valentine's Day are in a ceramic vase that she made in sculpture class. The pale yellow walls are papered with her paintings, abstract still lives and two female nude charcoals. Looking at them, you'd never guess that she whipped each one out the night before they were due. On Tuesday nights during sophomore year, I would convince her to go out with me by promising to stay up with her afterwards while she painted. We'd stumble back to our dorm at two in the morning, laughing about our two roommates who were trying to sleep in the other room. Regardless of how hard I tried, I'd pass out on the couch before the second song on any CD was over, while Lexie frantically scanned the crowded apartment for anything remotely artistic that she could paint. I'd wake up occasionally to hear Lexie singing along with familiar folk songs, her voice soft but soulful over top of the scratchy records. Somehow, she always finished by morning, and would carry the canvas that was twice the size of her body across campus while the paint was still wet.

The stairs creak as Lexie scampers down, wrapped in a maroon towel. She is holding something behind her back as she runs past me through the dining room and into the kitchen. She picks the magnet up off of the floor, shoots me a mischievous smile, and tacks up a photograph onto the refrigerator. "You're going to die when you see this," she sings as she hurries back upstairs.

I stand up and walk over, half out of curiosity and half out of obligation. It is a picture of her and Matt, the guy I've been seeing since October. I recognize that it is his room they are in, the familiar tapestries and Grateful Dead posters that plaster those walls. It is his bed they are sprawled across, her little body twisted around his. They are smiling. "Isn't that a riot?" She screams down from the top stair. I feel sick to my stomach as I try to remember a night when we were all together, taking pictures. I look closer, and notice that she is wearing a pair of his boxers and his favorite Phish shirt.

"When was this from?" I try to make the words come out evenly. I try to remind myself that this is a joke.

Lexie's voice from upstairs is muffled by the radio. "Oh, I guess it's from that night you stayed in to do that Shakespeare paper. I told you how we all stayed up all night playing poker, didn't I?" The whistling of her hair-dryer ends the conversation. I smell the chicken burning on the stove.

Step 5

Although Lexie doesn't appear to notice, the conversation at dinner is one-sided. I'm concentrating on eating while she tells me graphic stories about this manager at work whom she slept with. She loves to torture me with intimate details, knowing how boring my own sex life is. When Lexie lived down the hall from me freshman year, she would entertain all the girls on our floor during late night study breaks with her crazy sex stories. She would be waiting in my room for me on Sunday mornings when I had stayed out all night, eager to listen to gossip. She would curl up at the edge of my bed and prod me for details other than the replays of romantic conversation that I would happily offer. For three years I confided in her every detail of every hook up I had, but when I started seeing Matt I started to get offended by her personal questions. For two months she greeted me at the door with a hopeful, "Did you guys do it yet?" After many disappointments, she stopped asking, and now thinks of ways to hint around the subject. She just wouldn't understand if I told her that I knew he didn't love me, that he doesn't ever kiss me with the lights on, that recently we just fall asleep when I stay over. Both Matt and Lexie find my demands incomprehensible.

She pauses at the highlight of her current story, pouring herself more wine as if she can't precede without first calming herself down some. I forget to cover my expression of disgust. "Oh, did you want some?" She offers, and pours the last remaining sips into my empty glass. Lexie has not eaten anything, but has pushed around vegetables with her fork for ten minutes, between drinks. Apparently satisfied that I'm convinced, she reaches for her Camel Lights. "Carrie, that was great- I'm stuffed. So, where do you want to go tonight? I was thinking we could go to Calico's. Matt's band's playing there, and I'm sure he'd be hurt if you didn't at least stop by. I don't mind driving. I'm not going to drink tonight, I'm broke." She carries her full plate to the sink, dumping half of it into the dog's bowl and the other half down the drain. After six months of living here, she can never remember that we don't have a garbage disposal.

Step 6

There is nowhere to park at Calico's, so Lexie parks illegally on the busy highway. She puts her hazards on, and asserts, "They can't tow us now." We walk past the line of college kids that extends from the door to the road. Matt's Band, Grinch, always packs in crowds. Like every bouncer in Baltimore, this imposing jock at the door knows Lexie. The girls waiting whine as he lets us pass. As I walk in, I hear him cleverly explain, "Hey, they're with the band." I see Matt on stage immediately, his curly blond hair spilling over his face. He plays bass. I watch Lexie for a reaction, but she is already too busy talking to people I don't know. She motions me over and introduces me to two guys from her restaurant.

"What are you drinking, Alex? Wanna do a shot with us?" The short and stocky guy looks her up and down, winks at me, and tries to get the bartender's attention. "I know what you like," he says confidently as he flashes a twenty dollar bill.

Lexie pleads with me silently, and says to her friends weakly, "That's okay, I really wasn't planning on doing shots tonight."

The two guys laugh as the bartender takes their order. "Whatever, Ragdoll. We owe you a few," the other one says. Lexie gives me a hopeless shrug, and accepts what looks like whiskey.

Step 7

I have left Lexie and her friends from work at the bar, and am now pretending to be interested in Judy's dilemma over which lacrosse player to go to the prom with. I mean, Eric really has had a crush on her for the past two years, but she's been sleeping with Jack all semester. I utter my heartfelt sympathies to her and excuse myself to go to the bathroom. I spot many girls in line and think better of it, but it is too late. "Carrie! I've been looking all over for you." The woman's harsh Long Island accent reminds me of fingernails scratching a chalkboard. "Look at you--you look fabulous! That dress is so flattering, is it Ann Taylor?" I can't concentrate on anything she's saying because I am trying desperately to remember her name. How do I know her, anyway? I'm chugging my beer, nodding, when she grabs my shoulder and points. "That Lexie is such a scream-- a real riot!" Lexie has pushed her way to the front of the men's line, and is undoing her belt buckle.

I run over to her and grab her by the arm. The guy behind her pushes me away, saying, "Back off! Leave her alone." A chorus of men's room patronizers echo their agreement. Lexie is having problems standing straight already. Lately, she gets this way after only a few drinks- it used to take her fifteen. She ignores me and walks into the bathroom as one guy leaves smirking.

I refuse to run in after her. I can't keep babysitting. But how can I leave her alone in the men's room in her condition? I spot Matt's roommate John in line, and pull him aside. "Will you go in and check on Lexie?" I try to imitate the face Lexie makes when she wants something.

"Carrie, what do you want me to do?" He laughs like it's the most asinine request anyone's ever made of him, and it quite possibly could be. All of Matt's roommates have been witnesses to her at her worst before, though. He sighs. "Okay, okay, I'll save Lexie, but you owe me." As he pushes his way to the front of the line, I can't help but notice how good-looking he is. Or wonder if Matt would be jealous if I hung out with him.

Step 8

John and I have propped Lexie onto a bar stool, and have let her buy us a beer for helping her clean the puke off of her sweater. "That shot of Southern Comfort just didn't go down right." She acts utterly baffled by her sudden sickness. She has given the bartender her Visa card and is running up a tab for all of us. She is already five hundred dollars in debt to this credit card company, and has maxed out her Discover card, but I let her charge my drinks anyway. She had bought Matt a beer when she thought I wasn't looking, and brought it up to the stage in between songs. Did I imagine that he winked at her? No, I'm being ridiculous. She couldn't have done that to me- she was the one who set us up in the first place. They were always very flirtatious with each other, but she's like that with every guy. And she had been dating Matt's best friend Jeff. The four of us were inseparable for two months. When they broke up over Christmas, Lexie still hung out with me and Matt all the time. We're all just really good friends.

But all night, I haven't been able to forget the huge fight that Matt and I got in on New Year's Eve. He and his roommates had thrown a huge party, and three of my girlfriends from high school drove up from Philadelphia. I had promised myself I wouldn't get drunk- they were the kind of girls who would only drink wine coolers, and I knew they would be shocked at the crazy behavior of my new friends. I sat with them in the kitchen out of obligation, while as the hour neared midnight, Matt and Lexie and the others drank shot after shot. I surveyed the familiar scene with the eyes of a visitor- Matt and Lexie were always all over each other. I tried to think of an explanation when at midnight, he and Lexie were dancing. Three hours later, when Matt and I were alone in his room, I broke up with him. He told me that he had had enough of my condescending attitude, that I was no fun all night, that I probably wouldn't be later either. I stormed home to where my high school friends were already asleep, knowing that he'd forget it all by morning. Lexie stayed.

Lexie is behind the bar now, dancing with the fifty-year old bartender. Her favorite Doors song is playing, and she's screaming the lyrics and letting him pick her up and spin her in circles. When her feet touch the ground, she falls forward, her head into his beer gut. "Ragdoll," John, who is still sitting next to me, mutters as he shakes his head. He is the only other person in the bar who isn't laughing at her.

"You can't imagine what it's like," I hear myself saying to him. We split her gin and tonic and sit in silence, passing the glass back and forth until it's gone. Matt's band finishes their last song. I let John put his arm around me.

Step 9

Even though I saw that incriminating picture, even though I know Lexie had crashed at his place that night, I refuse to believe she'd do this to me. The worst part is that I'll never be able to confront her. If it happened, she'd lie about until the end. Or she'd fall back into her old routine-she had blacked out that night, it wasn't her fault. Matt knew how she got when she drank. God, does everyone know but me? I'm feeling more and more like the victim on a bad Melrose Place episode. If I'm ever going to find out anything, it'll be through Matt. He's a terrible liar- he's not a very smart guy, either. I excuse myself from John, who's in the middle of a conversation anyway, and search the crowd.

I see Matt alone, leaning onto the faux grain wood of the bar, ambitiously getting his money's worth from the five dollar all-you-can-drink-draft deal. His green baseball hat with the laughing, dancing bear ironed on the back is pulled low over his eyes, yet that unruly blond hair sneaks out from under it. He tilts back his head and swallows two last gulps of cheap beer, and waits for his empty glass to be filled. He scans the crowd frolicking below with a certain urgency. He's looking for me.

Suddenly a certain anxiousness overtakes him. He turns to his left looking frantically for someone to talk to. He shoots the bartender a look of desperation, silently pleading for him to begin a conversation. It is too late. I am walking straight towards him. I feel my determined brow furrow and put or forced, sarcastic smile.

I saunter right up beside him, and force myself to dangle my empty glass over the bar seductively. He doesn't look up to see me take a deep breath. He will only stare at my left hand, the five fingers painted a red so dark and dull that it looks brown, resting as close to his elbow as they possibly could without touching him. I accept my beer and surprise the bartender with my enthusiastically sweet smile. I shift my entire body to face the slumped over boy who refuses to look at me. "Happy Valentine's Day," I coo over-dramatically.

"Hey, what's up?"

"I saw you here all by yourself. Have you seen Lexie?"

His hand turns the color of my nail polish as he clutches the green bottle. He squirms under my persistent stare, showing me only the right profile his face. "No," he lies.

I laugh at his discomfort. "Oh, that's funny, I thought she might have brought the pictures she got back to show you. You're really photogenic."

He ignores me.

"How are Jeff and John?" Like I really give a shit about any of his roommates-they always pretended to be asleep and I know they were always trying to listen.

"Fine."

"I haven't seen you all week...I thought you would have stopped today, or called at least. Lexie's manager sent her roses." My voice trails off, challenging him.

The label from his beer bottle is completely torn off by now. He is tearing the damp paper and rolling it into little balls. "You know I hate these stupid holidays. I forgot about it until I got here and saw all these cheesy girls decked out in red. I'll buy you a beer, though." He looks at me and smiles right through me.

I hear myself laughing evilly. "No thanks, don't go out of your way or anything. I have to find Lexie anyway. Have you seen her?"

He shrugs and looks across the bar. "No, is she here?"

I had seen them talking at least three times. "Well,

Matt, she's here either passed out in the corner now, or looking for someone to pass out with, preferably someone who's supposed to want to spend time with me."

"What? Why are you being so sketchy? Is it because I haven't called? Listen, Carrie, I've been really busy- with hockey practice, the band, and I'm failing two classes-"

"At least you'll pass English. Didn't you get A's on those two papers I practically wrote for you? It's good to know you appreciate me, at least. I mean, what a good friend I've always been to you." My voice pierces the smoky air, and I feel my hands flipping my long hair mercilessly. I lean towards him and put my hand on his arm.

He finally turns to look at me, staring right at my plastic smile. "Stop it! Why do you have to make me feel so god damn guilty? It's not my fault, I never wanted it to be like this! What are we, anyway?"

My smile has electrically slipped to a disgusted smile. "I don't know- you've been perfectly happy to have it all your way. After six months, things evolve, or they just end. You can't keep being so fucking selfish-"

"Don't blame me for this. You don't know what the hell you want. Do you remember last weekend? The one time I need someone to talk to, and you couldn't even come over-"

"Yeah, come to think of it, you always could call at three a.m. Maybe just once, you could have stopped by in the daytime, somewhat sober at least, maybe if you could have kept your hands off my best friend-"

"Listen, Lexie and I have always been good friends- we understand each other. If you can't handle the fact that once in a while, I like to talk to someone who will listen to me, who isn't trying to make me into something I'm not, then you have a real problem."

"So is that why you couldn't send me a card today?

Were they all out of the 'Sorry I Fucked Your Roommate' variety? You're a bastard."

His lips are parted, as if there is something he wants to say, as if there anything he could say. For a brief moment, a look of pity crosses his face before he turns and walks away. It sobers me. I dig the heels of my black clogs into the thin, cheap carpet. I notice what feels like everyone I know eyeing me skeptically. I straighten myself taller and cross my arms to cover my heaving chest. I guess I never knew either of them at all.

Step 10

It's last call now, and I push through the laughing, drinking crowd to find the front door. I walk outside to find that there has been an unexpected snowstorm. The dull and dirty concrete of the city has been disguised in pure white. It's all a momentary deception, though. Tomorrow we'll have transformed it all into brown sludge.

Lexie is clearing the ice off of her windshield with her bare hands while sitting on the hood of her car. "Carrie, I have to drive home or I'll get a ticket." I'm impressed with how clear her sentences come out now that we are alone and she needs help. "Where are you going?"

Step 11

I am walking home alone now, since I have no money for a cab and am too stubborn to ask for a ride. I needed the fresh air anyway. I've felt that I've wanted to cry for the entire evening, but I won't give either of them the satisfaction. All I have to do is walk the remaining five minutes home, and then I can lock myself in my bedroom and write.

I turn off the main highway at the Exxon Station, making a right onto the alley way. The snow has framed all the familiar sights of impoverishment- the discarded thrift-store cardtables, baby strollers missing back wheels, and abandoned plastic toys on the front porches of the duplexes. I sing "Winter Wonderland" in my head as I walk; if the verse, ends when my right foot is forward, I'll make it home okay. If the verse ends with my left foot forward, I'll be raped any minute. I'm almost done with the entire song when I hear a car engine behind me. I try to run, but my clogs were not made for snow sprinting. I kick them off and feel the wetness instantly soak through my cotton tights to my bare kin. I run without turning around.

"Hey, wait!" The car pulls up beside me and a boy I recognize leans his lead out the passenger side window. "Aren't you Lexie's roommate? What are you doing walking by yourself at this time of night? Get in the car." His voice is stern.

I hop in the back seat silently. I stare at the city scenes that are rushing past me through the icy glass. The guy driving is wearing a Calico's shirt, and I remember now that he was the bouncer. He lectures me the entire ride to my street, as we pass cop cars and stray juvenile delinquents. He drops me off at the corner of my street. I don't say a word.

Step 12

I forgot to pick my clogs up from the alley. I am suddenly aware of the thinness of my dress, of how my soaked feet have made my whole body numb. I am one block from home. I fumble in my purse for my house keys, praying I didn't leave them in Lexie's car, and find her pack of cigarettes. I don't smoke, but I light one for the hell of it. I inhale and try to distinguish the puffs of smoke from my breath that is illuminated in the frosty air.

The front door of our house is wide open, and the frantic barks of our Dalmatian greet me from the porch steps. Lexie is sprawled out on the linoleum of the kitchen, holding the phone receiver in one hand, frantically pushing random buttons with the other. She lets both ends crash on the tile and looks up at me with watery blue eyes. "Carney, there you are." The words are slow and slurred together, sounding like a child's with a lisp. "I couldn't find you, and it snowed, and Matt said you were mad at us."

"Did he drive you home? I was worried, is all." She lets me hoist her off the ground and leans on me while we walk together to the couch. I try to help her take off the sweater that's covered in vomit, but she insists that she can do it. I close the front door and check the lock.

She is mumbling now. It's one of the rare nights when she doesn't get angry or violent, but talks of things that she'd never admit to in the morning- the father that hit her, the mother that she never wants to be like, her own weaknesses. Curled up into a ball, she takes up only one third of the couch. Her unruly hair covers her mouth and muffles the words. "Carney, you're so lucky... It's only sex, you know... they never care...nobody gives a shit...can't you see that?"

I walk from room to room, turning off all the lights, trying not to listen to her. I hang up the phone and notice that there are no messages. Finally, I turn her on her side and cover her with an afghan. She is sobbing and clutching the pillow. Her eyes are closed and she whispers, "You know, you're the best friend I've ever had."

I reach to turn off the last lamp, and stare for a moment at the painting on the wall beside it. It is a still-life of bottles, probably the only things Lexie could find to paint. Unlike most still lives, there is no light hitting the objects- the green of the glass is eerily distorted, the bottles strangely converged, swirls of darkness dancing like the dark water under a frozen surface of pond. I brush her hair back from her face, and leave the lamp on. I know that I will not be able to sleep when I go upstairs, and that I will check on her through the night to make sure she is still breathing. Before I walk away, I hear myself consoling her softly, "Shhh, it will be okay. Everything will be all right tomorrow."

Grown-Ups

Julie Weller

Tyler sat at the kitchen table, his twelve year old frame awkwardly huddled into the chair. From where he was sitting he had a perfect view of the storm raging outside. The sky was flat gun-metal gray, unbroken for as long as the eye could see. Through the illumination of the front porch light, Tyler watched the snow beat down in a smooth, hypnotic rhythm. In the background he could hear the high-pitched whistle of the tea kettle.

"Tyler!"

Tyler's body suddenly stiffened at the bark of his mother's voice. Heaving a sigh, he slowly unfolded himself from the chair and stretched as the tea kettle screeched incessantly.

"Tyler, get the damn kettle! Must I do everything around here?"

The boy heard a thump and recognized that to mean his mother was finally out of bed. He glanced at the kitchen clock and saw it was a quarter to four: his mother had just awakened.

"I'm coming to bring your tea, Mom," Tyler called up the stairs. "You decent?"

"What the hell kind of question is that? Just bring me the tea! I feel like I swallowed a freakin' desert!"

Tyler rolled his eyes, and caught a glimpse of the crack in the living room ceiling, noticing at how it was snaking its way up and back the length of the room. Someone was going to need to fix it.

Seeing his mother's door slightly ajar, Tyler knocked and gently shoved it open with the toe of his work boot.

"Took you damn long enough," the woman grumbled from her favorite armchair. "Good thing it wasn't an emergency! I'd be dead by now."

Tyler ignored her and went about fixing up her T.V. table. Avoiding her gaze, he handed her a steaming cup. "Drink the tea Mom, it'll help you wake up."

"You are such a dear, taking care of me like this," Caroline McViern conceded, patting her son on the hand. "I know I'm not the easiest person to live with Ty, but you're the man of the house now."

Tyler knew the routine by heart. His mother would rant and rave for awhile and then fall back into a stupor soon after. He would just have to wait it out.

"You're not like your father, God Bless us all for that!"

"Mom, just drink your tea," Tyler repeated soothingly. "Do you want me to open your curtains? It's snowing."

Tyler made a move to spread the thick drapes, but the sound of his mother's dry, rasping cough stopped him. He turned and watched as the woman bent low and flattened her chest against her bird-like thighs. Her thin shoulder blades were outlined by the ragged cotton housecoat she wore, seemingly, on a daily basis.

"Get me a hard candy or something Tyler, don't just stand there!" She croaked the words out, saliva darting from her narrow lips.

Tyler left her and when he returned, found his mother tipping a bottle of amber liquid into her steaming cup of tea. "Here," he said gruffly, shoving the peppermint into her pinched face.

"What's with you?"

For the first time that day, Tyler chanced a look into his mother's eyes. "Nothing," he answered lamely.

"What are you staring at? Didn't I ever teach you to mind your own business?" Caroline's voice had hardened, slurring over the word business. She looked about ready to strike her son. Tyler dropped and closed his eyes, trying to stamp out his mother's wild look.

"Oh I'm so tired all of a sudden," she complained, falling back into her chair. "I don't know why I never have any energy."

"I'll let you get some sleep Mom," Tyler whispered. But the woman had already lapsed into a deep slumber.

Lacking much energy himself, Tyler draped an old quilt over his mother and removed the clear bottle from her death-grip. He tip-toed out of the room, leaving the door open slightly. Pausing outside and resting his head against the wall, Tyler listened for the familiar wheezing breath of his mother. She wasn't going to awaken again for awhile. .

Sadly shaking his head, Tyler pushed himself off the wall and headed back to the kitchen. With an air of repetition, he dumped the contents of the bottle down the drain and washed out the sink. When the last of it had been cleaned out and the tea pot had been put away, Tyler collapsed onto his perch again. He sat mesmerized by the soft white flakes falling. He knew that the storm was not about to taper off soon. With a contented sigh, he cradled his brown head in the crook of his arm, cheek pressing against the cold Formica tabletop.

The complete lack of sound woke him up. He stretched like a house cat. The comforting hum of the refrigerator was absent and he detected no noise coming from his mother's room. She was still dead to the world.

"Aw damn!" he exclaimed in frustration. "The lights went out!"

Tyler checked his watch and the face glowed, illuminating the digital numbers. "Five-thirty! It's only five-thirty." He thrust himself up and walked over to the window. Twilight had set in and the snow had slowed, but the wind had created large drifts. He shuffled to a cabinet and pulled out a flashlight, testing it. A ring of deep yellow shone in his eyes, grew weaker and went out. Pawing through the various cups and half empty liquor bottles, he was unable to find more batteries. He moved to another cabinet and picked out the tallest of the used candles. Humming under his breath, Tyler set to work arranging it in the empty scotch bottle, a trick he had learned from his mother, and lit it.

Gathering a blanket around his shoulders, Tyler carried the candle into the living room and up to his mother's room. He leaned his ear into the door before peeking inside. His mother was still slumped in the easy chair, her head tilted in a painful angle. Tyler glided toward her and gently propped her head with a pillow. Caroline McViern didn't stir.

Biting back the urge to slap the drawn, pasty-white cheek, Tyler pivoted away from her and his eyes came to rest on the old wedding photograph on the bureau. The man and woman in the picture seemed so far off from who they were that day. Caroline McViern's eyes had been crystal clear. They were nothing like the ones he had stared into that afternoon. Broken blood vessels wove an intricate web through the whites of her eyes. Despite her problem, Tyler could not imagine having another mother. He still loved her.

Holding the melting candle, Tyler left the room and entered his own across the hall. His head was crowded with a mental slide-show of his life and he succumbed to it. Tyler curled himself under his blanket and watched the candle wax drip and dry on the cool bottle. His last conscious thought was of his ninth birthday party, the day his father left them, forcing Tyler to take over the role of care-giver. Tyler's face set into a grimace.

* * *

Each step in the over-sized boots, the only thing left of his father, was tentative and slow-going. Every few feet Tyler would have to yank his foot out of the thigh-high snow drifts and plod on. The boy paused, banging his gloves against his legs, attempting to crack the icicles that coursed through his veins, and hoping to wake up his hands and legs.

"Gotta keep going Ty," he encouraged. "No fun dying all alone in the snow."

A few paces later his foot sank down; irritated, he plunked his body onto the crusty snow. Through frozen eyelids hooded with a layer of exhaustion, Tyler studied his surroundings. The rural landscape, monotonous in the dry seasons, was now an unbroken plain of white that melted into the sky. Glancing south, he saw his deteriorating yellow ranch house poking up from the stark-white snow. Ten yards to his left was the mound of his mother's Chevy, laid to rest under a blanket of new snow. Even without the bad weather, the car had been stationary for the last month, due to a dead battery.

"Stupid piece of junk," Tyler grumbled. "It never worked right even before it crapped out."

Tyler's lamentations were cut short when he saw a dark figure bounding over the field from behind their dilapidated barn.

"What the hell?" He struggled to his feet. "Rusty!" he yelled, smacking his hands together. The sound was hollow and small in the empty terrain.

"Here boy!" A large black Labrador sprang over to the boy, pushing his front paws onto his chest, knocking him over. "Hey boy!" Tyler sputtered around the wet kisses. "Oh man, you smell like Callie! Were you hanging out with the Ryders' cow again?" Scratching him roughly behind the ears, Tyler joked, "You didn't scare her calf again did 'ya?" He affectionately added," Oh you dumb mutt."

Picking himself up from the indent in the snow, rejuvenated by his visitor, Tyler whistled low through the small gap between his front teeth and motioned for the dog to follow. Rusty bounced ahead, his small feet barely grazing the hardened surface and his dark coat dusted with snow. It wasn't too long before another farmhouse loomed up out of the horizon. Tyler noticed the swell of gray smoke as it boldly rose from the large brick chimney.

"Hurry up boy," Tyler called out to Rusty who had raced off to chase a jack-rabbit. "I betcha ol' Man Huller has some hot cocoa brewing. Let's get over there!"

Running as if stuck in a vat of thickened whipped cream, Tyler stumbled toward the old house. With a final burst of energy, the boy vaulted himself over the porch railing and sprawled onto the hardwood piling face-down.

"Well look who's here!" Emma Huller, a vivacious red-head, exclaimed from the front door. "Tyler McViern, what in the world are you doing on my front porch?"

Tyler's face burned as darkly as his maroon wool coat. He shyly met her piercing green eyes and fumbled mentally for something to say. "I, uh... I was just coming over to visit Mr. Huller. Uh, is that all right?" Tyler sheepishly picked himself up, brushing off his jeans.

"You're telling me you trekked through this stuff?" she asked, her Louisiana accent deepening with incredulity.

Tyler scuffed the toe of his boot on the floorboards and casually nodded his head. "It was really no big deal. I mean, I wasn't scared or nothin'. I'm used to this Wisconsin weather."

The older woman wagged her head, making the fiery curls shake. "Come inside Tyler, you must be half frozen by now!"

Without another word, Tyler followed her inside, catching her sweet smelling perfume mixed with the scent of fresh pie.

"Let me take your jacket, Tyler." She stepped over to him and touched his collar. "Grandpop is resting right now, but make yourself comfortable in front of the fire."

"You baking something? It sure does smell good."

"It's peach pie, right out of the oven. Want me to get you a slice?"

"Thanks, that would be great! Do you have something to feed Rusty?" Tyler jerked his thumb toward the dog curled on the hearth. "I'm not sure when he ate last."

"One large ham bone, courtesy of last night's dinner, coming up."

Tyler let out a smothered whistle of appreciation watching the sway of her hips as she gracefully exited. Unable to sit still in front of the fire, Tyler drifted over to study an old piano crowded into the corner of the living room. He traced his fingers over the yellowed ivories and smiled at the metal cylinder covered with markings that reminded him of Braille. He remembered a story Old Ferris Huller had told him about his player piano. He claimed that his grandfather had won it during a poker game way back when Lewis and Clark were traipsing around buying up land. Tyler recalled his completely falling for the story then, a naive and childish nine year old.

"I brought you some hot cocoa, too," Emma said, breaking into his reverie.

Taking the steaming cup from her hands, Tyler's heart raced like a marching band snare drum as their fingertips grazed. He quickly turned from her and walked over to the ancient gramophone. "What's your Grandpop's favorite song again, Miss Huller?" Tyler bent down low and spoke into the horn, his voice echoing back like the ocean in a sea shell.

The woman chided him. "Tyler, we're friends. Call me Emma!" She then continued in a serious tone. "Moonlight Serenade," was her reply to his question. She walked over to stand next to him. "When Grandma Penelope was still alive... you remember her, right?" Tyler nodded mutely. "Well, she and Grandpop would dance the night away to it. Whenever my Momma and I were up visiting from Louisiana, it always seemed that it was dancing time for them." She motioned her head toward the still form in the other room. "He would get up from the dinner table and say, 'Penny my love, I hear our song playing.' She would laugh and pretend to be shy until he put the record on. He hasn't listened to it since," she added, sighing.

Tyler sucked in his breath, uncomfortably aware of her body so close to his. "I liked watching them dance too."

"You were five when she died, weren't you?" Again he silently nodded. "I was fifteen and I still remember like it was yesterday."

"I really miss your grandma's cooking. She made the best Polish meatballs."

"She was good at a lot of things, but she was the best at loving Grandpop. No one could make him happier." Emma moved over to the wall covered with frames and old tin photographs, pointing to one. "Their wedding made headlines of the Wisconsin Tribune."

Tyler drifted over and saw what she was talking about. It was a framed copy of the 1944 edition of the Tribune. The banner read: "Wealthy Landowner Weds Local Immigrant." Underneath was a photo of the young couple exiting the church.

"Grandpop never once thought about her poor background." Emma clicked her tongue against her teeth. "He was so damn proud of her."

Tyler wandered over to the dining room where the old man lay sleeping in a rented hospital bed. The large table with its impressive chairs was shoved off to the side, making ample room for the temporary occupant. The gnarled, hairy fingers with cracked and blue-tinted nails loosely clutched a T. V. remote on his large stomach. Tyler noticed the re-run of M*A*S*H mumbling from the old black and white at the foot of the bed. Somehow the scene looked oddly untroubled to the boy, as if it was perfectly normal to have a dying man in full view of everyone.

"How's your mom, Tyler?" Emma asked softly, joining him in the entranceway."

He shrugged and stuffed his hands deep into his pockets. "I left her ranting in the dark when I came here."

"You lost your power?"

"Yeah."

"Why don't you and Rusty hang out here for awhile? She'll fall asleep soon."

Tyler nodded his head. "She always does."

As the late morning sun rose higher in the sky, deepening the shadows across the floorboards, Emma draped her arm around Tyler's shoulders, noticing how they were almost the same height. The two stood like that, the grown-up supporting the man-child, as the fragile old man lay unconscious and unaware. On the small screen, Klinger, proudly decked out in a pink dress and pill-box hat with a matching patent leather purse, pranced around Hawk-Eye and Major Houlihan as the tinny studio laughter crescendoed.

The Small Time

Laurence Ross

I glanced back to make sure that the sofa was still safely wedged in the bed of the pickup truck. The few street lamps lining the road put off a pale, orange glow against the leafless branches, and made it seem as if we were driving through a tunnel, complete with an ore-fractured ceiling. Stacy was zoned out in the driver's seat with thoughts of geometry or breakfast or road kill looping through her mind - the kind of things you never intend to think about but often do when behind the wheel of a car. Her straight red hair looked brown in the dark and her face looked whiter and somehow prettier. The radio was off but it seemed more awkward to turn it on and undo the silence between us. Ahead, Mark drove Tim's station wagon and our headlights silhouetted the recliner crammed sideways into the trunk.

The furniture seemed like a big deal. Usually we stole something like flowerpots from the outdoor garden center at Wal-Mart and used them to spell out K-Mart Rules in the empty parking lot. My mother said that it was depressing to see children so bored and at such a young age when surrounded by all of God's creation. But it was the unfortunate truth of our adolescence, and there would be no tornado to sweep us away to a more colorful existence. During a drive by last weekend, car lights off and horn blaring, we pelted the house where the angry old gas station owner lived with dusty pieces of plastic fruit, booty from the local diner. The apples and grapes landed softly on his lawn, creating small, shallow craters in the snow. Tim always suggested the same thing - pulling up For Sale signs and replanting them in houses further down the block - and although the rest of us never found the act itself that amusing, Tim's laughter was contagious.

But the furniture was large and obvious, and we looked like real robbers, at that hour and under those conditions, who had carted away the insides of a house while the family slept soundly upstairs. The truth was we'd hauled off items from the annual good-as-new sale in the church parking lot, an event organized and run by the old women who carried wooden rosaries and still received communion on the tongue. They geared up once a year to sell used crap in the name of charity. Integrated into the homily for the past six masses, Father Burton had urged the community to donate any unwanted belongings to church. Jewelry boxes covered with macaroni and glue, a dead uncle's brass harmonica collection and moth-ball infused lavender, grey and black dresses adorned with lace ruffles were piled in taped-up boxes outside the door to the rectory. Whatever hadn't been stuffed inside was lined up by the altar boys in the parking lot and covered in white tarps. We'd rifled through half-filled coloring books and semi-functional toasters in the dark, flashlights bouncing off of scratched antique wall mirrors, until we came upon the real prize: a green leather couch with only one cushion missing.

Up ahead, Mark slammed on the brakes and Stacy screeched to a stop behind him, the couch sliding into the cabin of the truck, arm against the window. Mark left the car running in the middle of the street as he got out and walked towards us. I saw the wry smile on Mark's face and wondered what sort of scheme he was concocting. Mark's brain functioned at a level somewhere between juvenile and delinquent, ever longing to just have a good time. Through a series of nondescript circumstances, Tim and I had become attached to Mark like a string of paperclips to a magnet, clinging to a confidence that we both lacked but nonetheless admired.

His long legs looked longer in the slanted shadows. His white T-shirt stood out in stark contrast to the deep bluish air, speckled with an occasional living room lamp or porch light. He hugged his arms to his chest and Stacy rolled down the window. The oddity of the situation struck me. Not the sin-stricken furniture in back, but that I was riding with Mark's girlfriend. If Stacy had been mine, she certainly wouldn't have been riding with Mark. Clearly I posed no threat to their relationship, and that depressed me. She leaned out the window to confer with Mark as I sat tilting the air vent toward the ceiling, then toward the floor, then back toward the ceiling again. The social structures of adolescence were written in inerasable ink, and Mark, Tim and I had been permanently and impenetrably fixed to each other, until Stacy had appeared.

Tim's station wagon puffed out thick white plumes of exhaust. He was fully reclined with his feet pressed up against the windshield. I watched his head bob from side to side, indicating that he was listening to the radio or at least hearing music in his head.. Residents of Middletown, Connecticut, under the age of 25 were doing at least one of three things at all times: one, sleeping; two, eating; three, trying to figure out a way to escape. Even the dogs went straight to their hair-covered blankets right after dinner. I shifted in the passenger seat, sure that we were being watched through the slits in some old woman's bedroom blinds. Alerted by prolonged activity after nine p.m., she would begin to panic and call her equally elderly neighbor who would peek out her own window, reach for the baseball bat wedged in her umbrella stand, and keep her eyes pasted to the street. Words like hoodlum and riffraff would be exchanged.

Calling my parents from the police station would have tethered my foot to Middletown forever. There would be no car for graduation, no college in warm, oh-so-far away Miami, no brief letters in the mail saying everything is fine and here is a little spending money. Two weeks before, my father had pulled me out of bed and dragged me downstairs to the dining room. My mother was holding a family meeting because my younger brother had been arrested. Chester was in the sixth grade. He and his best friend Anthony had gotten half way through writing their curse word on the wall of the library when the police happened to drive by. A large JUG was written in thick black marker across the stone wall. The officer stood over them and forced the two junior hoodlums to change the word to foolish before he shoved them in the backseat of the police cruiser. Chester said that Anthony cried.

My mother sat at the dining room table, wrapped in her bed robe, face flushed and eyes bloodshot. Her short hair stood straight up in the air as if she had spent a large portion of the morning pulling at it. Chester sat in a chair across from her, legs crossed beneath him, idly playing with a rubber band. My father was pissed about the graffiti fine. My mother half-screamed, half-wept a speech about how she had tried to raise good children. She began to 1 list the ways as if she had to prove it to herself. Hadn't we been made to rake the leaves for Mrs. Marley next door? Hadn't we been shoved into elf costumes every Christmas to help Santa distribute toys to the children at the hospital? Every year she made us valentines to give to our teachers. Then suddenly, her youngest child was on a collision course with alcohol addiction, a convenience store robbery and friends named Diesel and Axe. Chester was forced to draft a handwritten essay to the police commissioner about the proper use of the magic marker, while my mother, who forced us all to sit there while Chester wrote the damn thing, moderated a family discussion on the meaning of "community respect."

"We're going to the park," Stacy announced, rolling up the window against Mark and the cold.

"What for?" I asked.

"Because that's where Mark wants to go."

"It's just going to be cold and I hate the park. We may as well go to Tim's basement and watch you and Mark make out all night."

"And you could sit there and stare as usual," said Stacy, focused on the car in front of us. She reached to turn the heat to its highest setting, and I wished I had kept my mouth shut.

My mother always told me to never go to the park after dark because that was the time people were surprised by drug dealers, kidnappers and men with knives. I doubted that my mother had ever seen a marijuana leaf, much less an actual drug dealer, but she was also the person who inspected the shrubs that surrounded our house with a flashlight before going off to bed. She liked to think that no one noticed. As if anyone, even the dimmest elderly neighbor, believed my mother was merely walking the dog around the house a few extra times. Sometimes it was not even completely dark when she wandered around the garden, leash tight in hand.

In actuality, the only miscreants we had ever encountered in the park after dark were naked people, couples rolling around on the wooden footbridge among their discarded clothes or kids meshed together on a bench, adding their initials to the dozens already there. That fall, our headlights had illuminated two naked girls running around in a circle on the open field. They were girls, not women, one with a wide face and a body that spread in the hips and the other with nearly no distinguishable curves and short hair. They wore only socks. Shielding their faces from the light, they dropped to the ground and began to slither towards the trees on the other side of the park, like slippery fish trying to make their way upstream.

I wondered what Stacy looked like naked, if she would look the same as those two girls, pale and washed out in our beams of light. Would she have dropped to the ground, embarrassed by exposure? It seemed like she would have stood there and stared back, right into the blinding glare.

The blasting heat had dried my mouth. Why couldn't I be in the station wagon with Tim listening to Buddy Holly sing "That'll Be the Day?" A cloud pulled over the nearly full moon, making the sky significantly darker. Stacy was slouched forward and her face looked placid, sliding in and out of the dim street lamps. I looked up but could find no end to the cloud.

We pulled up to the green chain-link fence that half-surrounded the park. "Well, let's get started," Mark said as if we were workers for Habitat for Humanity. He popped the trunk of the station wagon while Tim struggled into his sneakers. "You two get the couch." Mark had his jacket on then and he grunted under the weight of the heavy chair.

"What are we doing?" I always had to ask.

"Playing house."

I was not really expecting an answer. Or an intelligible one anyway. Playing house reminded me of kindergarten children in oversized aprons, playing with frying pans the size of a chocolate chip cookie.

Stacy hopped onto the bed of the truck, unlatched

the hatch and propped herself between couch and cab, feet right below the window. "So are you going to help or what?" she said, pushing. The couch slid forward and tipped off the truck into the mud. I turned around hoping to switch jobs with Tim or I Mark, but Mark was already halfway across the field, an end table tucked under one arm a desk lamp in his hand. I didn't even know we took those. Tim wasn't far behind, pressing toward the strip of trees like an armadillo with the recliner hefted up on his back. Stacy and I hoisted the couch, heels in slush, and I felt like I was part of a desert caravan, only it was cold, and there was snow in my shoe.

The field was a camouflage of dirt, snow and dead grass. The No trespassing sign had been uprooted long ago and thrown into the creek where it still lay rusting - one end below the surface of the water and the other jutting out, polished white with snow. Mark had once stolen Mora Comely's bicycle while she was darting about at field hockey practice. She turned to see him riding it right into the creek and went screaming after him, crying. When she finally caught up, she found the bike partially submerged on a bed of rocks with suds and debris slowly filtering in the spokes of the wheels. Mark cautioned against tattling, threatened to spread a rumor that she was a slut, and after Mora pulled her bike from its wet bed of deteriorating soda cups, unrolled condoms and a slush of cigarette butts, the matter was never brought up again. Mora walked home with brown stained sneakers and a swollen face.

Mark adjusted the lamp on the end table. "Too bad there aren't any outlets out here."

Tim plopped onto the recliner, pushed the footrest forward, and stretched his arms up and over his head. "What took you guys so long?"

Mark positioned the sofa parallel to the chair and

pulled Stacy down on top of him. They took up two cushions. That left me the end. Cold metal coils pressed upwards under the worn fabric as we sat in silence. Tim used a stick to draw lines in the mud, oblivious to the awkward lack of conversation. A cold wave moved through my body and I realized that I was nervous again. Uneasy silences made me anxious, I was a wreck cutting class, always looking over my shoulder, arriving home in the afternoons expecting a phone call from the principal and a lecture from my mother. Saturday mornings I shot up in bed. Was it a Tuesday? Had I overslept? No time for a shower, run!

Mark and Stacy kissed quietly beside me. There was a slit in the arm of the sofa so I stuck my hand into the hollow space. Any stuffing that might have been there was missing. A beam of headlights washed over the scene, our living room in the woods. The police. An essay: The Proper Placement of Furniture. The white cars would come speeding across the field, red and blue pouring over the blanched ground and illuminating the dark tree branches, Mark's hand on Stacy's bare lower back. Cocky nightshift officers on too much caffeine with too little to occupy themselves would step out of their cars with black nightsticks and fur-collared jackets. This was all here when we got here, officer. That wouldn't work. Mark would suggest that someone must have mistaken the park for a dump. Tim would ask the officers if they'd ever shot anyone, and if, just for laughs, they had ever pulled water guns instead, you know, just for laughs. This would lead the cops to the clear conclusion that Tim was stoned, that we were all stoned, and after a thorough search of our vehicles, would link the unusual amount of loose change in our ashtrays with a recent laundromat robbery. During the whole search, Stacy would just sit there silently, not letting anyone know what she was thinking and Mark's hand would be resting on her knee. I sat very still, watching the car, resisting the urge to flee blindly across backyard fences, then calmed myself as the lights passed and the trees went dark again. Probably just some guy whose pregnant wife had sent him out for sharp cheese. My ear was suddenly burning, then cold and wet.

"We're not setting off fireworks out here; so who's going to see?" Mark laughed. I wiped the slushy snow from my face. "Take the stick out of your ass, man."

"So what are we going to do?" I asked. A plane passed overhead, red and white lights blinking a straight line across the sky. Aisles too narrow, knees against the flip-down tray, seats reclining a pathetic eight degrees. I wondered where the passengers were headed and if any of them were awake. I thought about the word Connecticut: connect, a reference to the state's role as a bridge between everything south of Pennsylvania and those sections of New England that people actually want to get to cut as in "someone please cut my pinkie off because there's nothing more entertaining around here than a Friday-night trip to the ER"; and finally, the lonely little i stuck in the middle.

"I'm bored," Mark said, which seemed unfair for the boy with the girlfriend to say. "Let's go to the playground." He had his arm around Stacy's waist, bunching her coat into ripples. She had one leg up on the back of the couch. Her hair covered the back of her neck and I wondered if my neck would be warmer if I had long hair. The picture was disturbing.

Tim pulled his hat down over his eyes - whatever spelled out in big white letters across the front. "I'm too lazy," he admitted.

Mark and Stacy wandered toward the playground, holding hands. Outlines of monkey bars, metal slides and swing sets stood out like skeletal beginnings, the framework of something incomplete and abandoned.

I stretched out on the sofa and looked up at the sky. The moon shone through a tiny tear in the clouds, reminding me of a very tired eye. Or maybe. God was glaring at us. I wondered if it was going to rain. It was cold, but not cold enough for snow. What would the first kid who came to the park in the morning think when he saw a living room set up next to the jungle gym? What did the mean man that owned the gas station think when he found all that plastic fruit strewn across his snowy lawn? The furniture would be ruined and it was difficult not to feel guilty. Maybe I would go to church on Sunday and bring a ten-dollar bill for the collection to even things out. I looked over at Tim who was also looking at the sky. He had spun around so that his feet were slung over the back of the chair while his head rested on the retractable footrest.

"So what do you think of Stacy," I said.

"I don't know. What do you mean?"

"You know, like, what do you think about her? Hanging out with us and stuff."

Tim clapped his shoes together, allowing the slush in the treads to fall on . the head of the recliner. "She's a girl," he said, like it was the start of a list that he forgot to continue.

"And?"

"She has boobs?"

I was pretty sure Tim's eyes were closed. He began to hum John Denver's "Leaving, On a Jet Plane."

"Remember those naked girls that we found that one time?" Tim asked while drumming his fingers on the arms of the chair.

"Yeah." Naked girls, spinning in their mesmerizing spiral, their own mix- ture of ring around the rosy and

Wiccan ritual.

"Do you think that they ever came back?" He paused trying to think of the answer to his own question. "I wonder where their clothes were stashed."

"I don't know." I looked at the spot in the field where the naked girls had danced. There was nothing but a trail of our footprints. Mark and Stacy had disappeared somewhere in the distance and shadows of the playground. "Why do you think they were wearing those socks? I mean it's not like they weren't already naked."

"Maybe they didn't want to step on a slug."

"I guess. But then they rolled on the ground."

"Yeah, but that was after we came."

What kind of jobs did such girls grow up to have? Teacher? Mother? The ice-cream scooper who offered extra sprinkles on cones? Would I recognize them on the street, fully clothed, flipping through a magazine in a drugstore aisle, leaning against a railing outside the mall, or sipping cream soda with their boyfriends outside the ice-skating rink?

The clouds had shifted again. Moonbeams lit up the sky like an x-ray, exposing thin edges of grey clouds surrounding deep blue splotches where the clouds grew thicker like old scabs. Mark and Stacy were dark blobs at the swing set. Stacy was talking to Mark but we were too far away to hear what was being said. I wondered what they talked about. What would I talk about with Stacy? Biology class, the sex organs of flowers, the intertwining of the pistil and the stamen among the petals, a theory or two about how Mr. Headly, the Spanish teacher, had lost his leg and what he used to do before teaching.

Mark hung on to the chain of a swing while leaning against Stacy. I could not tell if they were kissing but supposed that they had to be.

The car would be freezing again by the time Mark

was ready to leave. I would ride home with Tim no matter what. Mark pushed Stacy on the swing as she kicked woodchips in the air. The scraping of her shoes against the ground echoed slightly in the open night. She swayed and 1 thought of the pendulum of the grandfather clock in my living room, swinging bronze behind the little glass door. Both Stacy and Mark looked older farther away. Their rounded features were undefined. The chain twisted a little and Stacy crashed into Mark on the downswing, kicking him back into muddy slush. Tim laughed loudly. Though it was dark, 1 knew that Mark's expression was angry. Tim's cackle was so loud that every person in every house bordering the park must have heard. Tim's laugh probably carried even farther than that. He shook so hard that he looked like he was going to topple out of the chair. Stacy sat on the swing staring at Mark, her momentum reduced to a slow sway.

Moving fast, another car drove by and lit up the park in a spectrum of sharply contrasted grays. I once dreamt I was flying over a grey world, between grey clouds and grey buildings. People were toned in black and white and looking up at the sky. I started to plummet quickly yet was very aware of each instant of freefall as if something was resisting my descent.

The snow in my sneaker had melted, soaked my sock, and had begun to freeze again. I knew that when I took my sock off that night, my foot would be white and wrinkled. It would hurt to stand in the shower.

Tim dropped me off in front of my house, an ice-cube in an ice-cube tray of a neighborhood. During the week the sun had melted most of the snow from the week- end before, revealing patches of dead things all over. It had eaten holes in the snowy spreads that covered the roofs, all slanted in the same direction. Our flower boxes looked vacantly ugly again, plastic wrappers and wadded paper had reappeared in the r gutters. The half-eaten bird that my father had refused to dispose of, despite my mother's constant pleading, had resurfaced inch by inch on the front porch. The walkway was a frozen stampede of boot prints.

Chester was slumped on the couch, the house dark except for the flashing activity of the muted television.

"What are you doing?" I asked as I wandered behind the couch. I Love Lucy played on the television in black and white.

"Thinking of sixteen ways to solve world hunger. What do you think I'm doing?" Middletown's most-wanted was watching sitcoms, biding time until the next opportunity for petty crime presented itself.

"There's no sound."

"I didn't want to wake mom up. She'd come down and tell me that I should be sleeping and not wasting my time watching stupid shows that only people with meaningless, boring lives have time to watch. Besides, I've seen this one already."

Lucy was a tragic character; her strongest trait, that flaming head of red hair, quelled by the limitations of film and technology. Lucy, Ricky, Fred, and Ethel thrown together in an apartment building, friendship forged by proximity. Even Fred, who no one really liked that much, was not rejected. I wondered which bed Little Ricky had been conceived in, and if Stacy and Mark had squeezed into his twin yet. I wondered whether or not they climbed in naked or waited until they were under the covers to slip out of their clothes.

A trail of grey tread marks led from the front door, staining a path of dark wet blue on the carpet. I had forgotten to take off my shoes. I wrestled out of my coat and threw it on the arm of a chair. The picture frame on the mantel was streaked with glare. Inside my mother and father played bride and groom, she, though posed, looked completely comfortable, relaxed even, in the brown tones of the print. My father, on the other hand, stood rigid, adding a strange element of precise geometry to the picture, shoulders perfectly perpendicular to the spine, lips parallel to the shoulders. Only his eyes held a glimpse of estranged emotion. Yet oddly enough they fit together, like an apple and a steel core-remover - an unnatural yet logical combination.

"What did you do tonight?" Chester said without taking his eyes away from the screen.

"Nothing." Lucy wailed on the kitchen counter, palms slapping down in over-exaggerated swings, like treading water. Her face stretched in a frozen whine as she looked at each person in the room waiting for a reaction.

"Sounds riveting."

"Just as fun as your night, I'm sure." The television was our mirror, bouncing the conversation off the set so that eye contact was unnecessary like two people looking straight out the windshield of a car, united by a shared vision.

Outside, the street shone suddenly with the reflection of oncoming head-lights. A car came into view and pulled next to the curb in front of my house. The police had somehow tracked me down. I would be arrested in front of my younger brother. My mother would come scurrying down the steps in her nightgown and curlers, all set to give a speech about guests after eleven before realizing exactly who the company was - then she'd put her hand over her mouth and run up the steps to get my father. I would go to court and be sentenced to some private military school and excommunication.

The engine cut off and a car door slammed shut. The knocker fell in three quiet taps. I flipped the switch for the porch light and opened the door wishing for a girl scout, an evangelist, an employee of corporate America asking for participation in a survey about hair dyes and animal testing, or a member - of a newly formed political party handing out buttons reading change for the better in blocky green letters. Stacy stood alone, blinking under the high- powered porch light.

"Hello," I said, opening the storm door and stepping outside as if it were three in the afternoon. The frosted windshield of my father's station wagon gleamed like a sheet of scratched acetate. In only fifteen minutes, my body had forgotten how cold it was. "Hi," Stacy said.

Her red hair, which had seemed brown all night, was rich again in the bright light of the porch lamp. Her unzipped coat hung stiffly off her body and she moved a gloved hand toward her neck.

"So what are you doing here?" I asked, incapable of nonchalance. It seemed like a logical question. After all, we had sat on stolen furniture, exchanged mundane small talk that would be forgotten by morning, watched to see if anyone else was letting signs of frostbite show through their cool exterior. Mark was overly annoyed at Tim for laughing at his fail. We left the virtual living room set up in the park - no one willing to put forth the effort of returning the items to the church. I rode home with Tim; Mark rode home with Stacy. As far as we could tell, we were all going to go to sleep, wake up tomorrow and still be in Connecticut.

"You left your wallet in my truck. I thought you might want it back." She held it out. The wallet was bright blue nylon with a Velcro strip to keep it shut.

I was sure that Mark had brooded in a wake of incongruity sitting next to Stacy, pounding through radio stations, running down a list of our evening's deficiencies. Or maybe he had insisted on driving Stacy's truck, the tires found a patch of black ice, the hood a tree... But the truck sat right there in the driveway, gleaming lines of white salt reflected on the black paint.

I scanned the street for a moment. "Thanks," I said dumbly, shoving the wallet into my pocket. I wanted to go inside and get my coat. I glanced back through the storm door and saw Chester munching away at a newly opened box of vanilla wafers. "You could have dropped it off tomorrow. There's nothing inside it anyway. It's kind of just for show."

"It's no big deal." She moved her head slightly to look past mine. "Parents up late?"

"No. My little brother."

"Mark was telling me about him. He said he was cooler than you are."

I looked at her blanched face under the harsh porch light, her hair casting a grainy shadow over her pale cheek. I tried to smile but couldn't keep eye contact.

"I was just kidding," Stacy said and her lips curved slightly upward in a thin smile.

I tried to think of something to say - not school, not Mark.

"So where's Mark?" If anyone was awake watching us they must have wondered what we were doing, standing on the small porch not speaking, freezing to death. Perhaps a secret rendezvous, a girl in need of - in need of what? Answers for the chemistry test, a joint, a way to make her boyfriend jealous, love, sex, good conversation. My mother would claim the drugs were moving from the park to the heart of the neighborhood if she saw that same scene enacted across the street.

"I dropped him off," she said.

Stacy didn't move. Maybe she had tucked a note in the folds of my wallet - a love note complete with little doodles, the kind everyone saw passed between the seats on buses or handed off in the busy hallways of every high school. I wanted to have a conversation like adults did. Can you believe she is blowing off the carpool again? He didn't pick up his part of the bill as usual. I'm glad my kid doesn't do that, Let s get together for dinner on Friday at that new place on Johnson Street. But we were not adults. 1 considered bringing up I Love Lucy, a comical situation we could both pretend to laugh at. But laughing was so much easier with Chester or Tim. Burps, farts, general ignorance, an insult or a fault. Anything that pertained strictly to our masculinity - or jeopardized it - held potential for hilarity. Stupidity was supposed to be funny, like Lucy defrosting a turkey in the bathtub and getting a leg stuck in the drain, causing a flood in the bathroom.

The fire station let go an echoing siren that seemed to float across the sky in a rhythm of long breaths. The wails climbed up again and again only to be let back down. If something was happening in Middletown at that time of night, it must have been the end of the world: I should have reached for her hand, kissed her on the forehead, fumbled myself toward some astonishing physical decla- ration but 1 stood planted on the ~ icy welcome mat.

"I should go," Stacy said, staring at me for a moment before turning back toward her truck. Her hair slowly faded back to brown a~ she walked, securing one foot on the glazed path before lifting the other. She opened the truck door and disappeared into the interior. The engine revved, the headlights flicked on, and she drove away.

I opened the foggy storm door. Chester was sleeping on the couch or at least pretending to. I Love Lucy had ended.

"Well that wasn't very interesting," Chester said in a muffled voice, eyes closed. I ignored him because anything 1 said would only prompt a laugh from him, obnoxious and grating like the truth tearing. There was an infomercial for a stain remover on the television. A woman with blonde hair poured a glass of red wine on her blouse without flinching. The gesture was so matter of fact; it was hard to believe the infomercial was real and not created solely as a late-night comedy show for the lonely insomniac. No sound came out of her mouth but she looked very happy, as if she should have started splashing herself with burgundy years ago. I turned back toward the storm door and drew a shape in the wet fog with my fingertip - some formless creature like a deflated jellyfish. Then I erased it with a swipe of my palm, clearing a window to the dark of the other side.

Bagpipes

Margaret Dougherty

Her father was the only person who could ever over-hear her say "laced with" and honestly believe she was talking about lingerie or a decoration or some kind of arts and crafts project. She stopped mid-sentence when he stepped into the room, widening her eyes innocently. He put her folded laundry on the bed beside her, and smiled, before slipping out of her bedroom into the hallway without saying a word.

"Elle?"

"Yeah, yeah—sorry. My dad came in."

"Jesus, Elle, lock your door."

My father didn't believe in locks. He thought it made the house seem too sectioned, too territorial. But he did believe in privacy, and Elle knew he would have knocked had he no been carrying a large basket of darks. But that was too much to explain to Erin. Elle responded slowly, suddenly distracted.

"Yeah...next time."

"Well anyway...it was laced with something?"

"Yeah...hey, listen I've got to go. I'll call you later."

"What? Tell me first. Tell me what it was..."

Elle put the receiver down gently. She ran her index fingers across her eyes, up to her temples, and through her hair. Erin would call back in a few minutes, Elle knew. If she didn't answer after two rings her father would pick up, though he knew if it were actually for him it would only

be a foreigner selling windows or a local firefighter looking for pledges. Elle fell back against her pillows, exhaling as she glided backwards. Seeing her father made her
want to be what he thought she was. Seeing her father as
she told Erin what was laced with made her feel intense
guilt. He didn't know her and she was all she had.

She pushed herself off the down comforter and
walked towards the door. Flicking off the bedroom light,
she stepped into the hallway. Her dad hated wasting elec-
tricity. If her bedroom light was on and Elle wasn't in the
room, he would make sure she knew it. In high school,
he had, on occasion, called her cell phone just to let her
know. Leaving the light on in the laundry room was the
worst offense. The light steps at the top of the steps had
broken years ago, while her mother was still alive. To turn
it off you had to feel your way down the stairs, then reach
through the thick darkness until you found the thread-
like string connected to a sole light bulb.

In the kitchen, her father shook a frying pan with
his left hand and stirred noodles with his right. They
squirmed in the boiling water. In the pan, vegetables
sizzled. He had learned to cook the hard way—Elle
could attest to that—by trial and error. For the first few
months after his wife died, the meals were either burnt or
frozen. Some nights he would cook a whole burnt meal,
they would pick at it silently until they made eye contact,
and then they would order a pizza.

Now, just over two years later, stirring and frying,
Keith looked like a master chef. Elle had to laugh when
she walked into the kitchen, the door swinging on its
hinges behind her. The phone rang before she could say
anything. She stood at the counter, on the opposite side
of the bar, and watched her father. He lost thirty pounds
after her mom died, and he looked trim and younger that
Elle ever remembered him. His short brown hair was

speckled with small tufts of gray. He looked up at her, and smiled, his eyes squinting as he did so.

"You want to answer the phone?" My hands are full."

"Nah. It's just Erin again. I'll call her back."

They don't have an answering machine. Keith had broken their last one, and neither had ever thought to replace it. But there was something about an unanswered phone that made her dad nervous. Elle's mentality was—let it ring, they can call back.

"Here, stir this. Shake this."

"It's Erin, dad. Tell her I'm not here. Or something."

It would be the "or something." The man didn't lie. Elle could never understand that—her mother would lie about anything. She told telemarketers that she was the live-in maid, she told the grocery store employees that Elle was her sister. She loved to lie. Never about anything serious, only about fun stuff. Her dad got to the phone between the third and the fourth rings.

"Hello?"…"Oh, yes, hello Erin. How are you?"

Elle shook her head. He lived for small talk. Anyone who called for Elle got the "how are you?" the "What's new?" or the "tell me what's going on with you." Most of her friends knew to hang up when she didn't answer after two rings if they didn't want to get stuck on the line with her father. But Erin was a college friend, her roommate of three years, and wasn't used to calling Elle at her house.

"Well that's great, Erin. And the family is doing well?"…

"Wonderful. Well you tell them all I say hello."…

"Great."…

"Elle? Well actually, we're just about to sit down for dinner. Would it be alright if she called you a little later?"…

Well, I'll give her the message. Have a good night."…

"Ok, bye."

Keith put down the receiver and looked at Elle. She was distracted by the vegetables in the frying pan. It struck him how grown up she was. Her lean body pressed against the counter top, her dark hair spilled below her chest in soft lines. Her skin was darker than her mother's, lighter than his.

"Why'd you put peppers in?"

"Don't you like peppers?"

"I'm not in the mood for them tonight."

"Well just pick around them."

She looked at her father. The first few months after her mom died she couldn't make eye contact with him. There was a pain behind his eyes that was deeper than hers. There was a part of her that was jealous because his pain was different, more intense. It was irrational jealousy, she realized later. And after those first few months, the jealousy changed to relief when she realized that she'd find complete happiness again. Then it was guilt, because he never would.

"Set the table please, Elle."

She slid open the third drawer under the oven, and pulled out two place mats and napkins. They matched. These were a set her mother had picked out. Once on the table, the place mats and napkins blended into the scheme of the kitchen. Light blues and whites, highlighted with orange and yellow accent pieces. Her mother had loved bright colors. In any other house, the room may have looked like a kindergarten classroom. But not in Shelley's house. Somehow, because it was hers, it was okay, it was even stylish.

Elle poured herself a glass of milk, and an iced tea for

her dad. She sat at her place at the table, watching him silently. He turned the gas down on the range and let the vegetables simmer as he strained the noodles. From her seat at the table, nearly level with the frying pan, Elle could see small bubbles of grease flying out of the pan into the air, disappearing into the background of light blue.

Her father pulled the pan off the range, and poured half of the steaming vegetables onto one plate of noodles, the other half onto the next. With a look of satisfaction he walked towards Elle.

"Dinner is served."

"Looks good, dad. Looks good."

As soon as he placed her plate in front of her, Elle began sifting through he noodles and vegetables, trying to pull out the peppers.

"Hey, Grace. Let's not forget."

Elle put her fork down, and looked at her father apologetically. He wasn't a particularly holy man, but Grace was his thing. She remembered those nights saying Grace over food that hadn't quite thawed in the middle, or was blackened everywhere but the very center. Those dinners had been what brought the two closer. It was the one aspect where their pain was identical, at least as Elle saw things. Nothing else compared.

"...from my bounty through Christ, our Lord. Amen."

Elle always let her father say Grace. It was his, so she let him have it all to himself. He didn't mind. It made him feel like the head of the family, however small that family may be. She watched him lean over his plate. He always cut the noodles, something Elle and her mother used to tease him about. He chopped the vegetables and noodles into small pieces, balancing them dangerously on his fork, before moving his whole face forward to trap the food. Elle had tried countless times to teach him how to spin his fork until the noodles wrapped tightly. She knew he could do it, but for some reason he didn't want to.

Dinner was never long when it was just the two of them, which it usually was. Both Keith and Elle were fast eaters. Shelley had been the fastest of the three of them when she was alive. Something in Elle made her keep eating fast, keep carrying on an impractical trait—flaw—of her mother's. Those were the things that kept her real in some abstract way. Even the flaws. Especially the flaws.

The phone rang just as Elle finished the last of her noodles. Her plate was empty, aside form the line of peppers framing the edge. She got to the phone just after the second ring.

"Hello?"

"Hey! It's Erin. You finished eating?"

"Erin, I'll call you back. We're still eating."

That was a lie. She turned as her father's chair moved against the linoleum floor. He leaned over, grabbed the plate, and then pulled his from the table as well. Elle hated to leave him at the table alone.

"Elle, don't worry about it. I'm finished. I'll take care of the dishes. You go talk."

"Elle? Elle? Are you still there?"

"Yeah. I can talk. Hold on."

As she walked out of the kitchen, Elle squeezed her father's arm, and winked at him. The unspoken thank you. She took the stairs two at a time and burst into her room, slamming the door innocently behind her. She said nothing until she was comfortably on her bed.

"Hey."

"Hey? Elle, come on. You know what I want to hear."

Elle knew exactly what she wanted to hear. Erin had

left for Christmas Break two days before her. She wanted to hear all the details of exactly what happened, with who, with what, where, and when.

"What?" "Elle!"

"Er, it was fun. We all hung out. There were only a few of us left on the floor, so it was chill."

Elle had called Erin in a fit of excitement early this morning as she waited for the train home. She didn't have time for the details. She left her hanging with "I'll call you when I get home." Elle lived close to Philadelphia, where she went to the Art Institute and studied sculpture. Her dad was overly supportive, trying to compensate for the fact that he saw no possibility of a profession resulting from the study of making shapes out of clay. If Shelley had been alive, he would have been the voice of reason, pushing her to study something with substance. Elle knew this, though the two rarely spoke about it, and never directly.

This afternoon when Elle stepped into the empty house in Paoli, the phone was ringing. She didn't bother answering it, and instead plopped onto the sofa couch in the family room. Her father was still at work. When he came home and hour later, he found his baby, all grown up, asleep on the couch.

"Elle."

"What Erin?"

"What's the problem? Why won't you talk to me?"

"I'm sorry. I'm tired."

A lie.

"Elle, you were so excited about it. Just tell me and I'll stop bothering you."

There was a stinging hurt in Erin's voice, and Elle tried to retract her ealier annoyance.

"You're not bothering me. I'm tired. Sorry. Okay. So, Friday, after you left, we smoked. I have no idea what it was laced with, but Erin, it was out of control."

"Are you sure it was laced with something?"

"Erin, it was white."

"The pot?"

"Yes. White pot."

"Elle."

"Erin."

"That's crazy."

"I know. Er, I can't explain it."

"What else happened?"

"Honestly, that's pretty much it. Three nights of that…"

It was fairly painless for Elle to tell Erin the news, and it finally shut her up. They talked for another twenty minutes. Every five minutes or so, Erin would stop mid-sentence and double-triple-quadruple check—white?

"Listen, Er, I've got to go. I haven't really gotten a chance to talk to my dad much since I've been home."

"Alright, Elle."

"So I'll talk to you soon, alright?"

"Sounds good. Oh Elle! I completely forgot to tell you. I'm gonna be back in Philly tomorrow to do some shopping with my mom. I'll call you? Lunch maybe?"

"Tomorrow? You just left three days ago."

"It's only forty-five minutes away and my mom likes to shop at Liberty Place. So I'll call you?"

Keith sat in front of the TV, staring directly at the changing images but not taking much in. When Shelley was alive, he never watched TV. They talked for hours after dinner about anything, Keith sipping on a gin and tonic, Shelley a vodka and cranberry. She loved vodka. Keith had never seen a woman drink vodka as well as his wife. Every drink she ordered had at least a half shot of the clear syrup. In college, he watched her down shots

from a five-dollar bottle of Stalingrad. She had graduated to Kettle One before she died.

A door closed upstairs. He couldn't be sure, but it
sounded like the hollow slam of the bathroom door. Elle
always slammed doors behind her. He had tried to break
her of the habit, but it never stuck and it was one of his
few pet peeves that he had surrendered to her. He had
surrendered other things to her. He let her go to art
school to study sculpture. Sculpture? He wanted her to
be happy. But he didn't want her to be homeless.

There were times he wondered if she cared either
way. Last August, over dinner, he asked her what exactly
someone does when they graduate with a proficiency in
sculpture.

"You sculpt, dad."

He focused all his energy on being inquisitive—not
condescending.

"Yes. Alright. What are you going to sculpt?"

"I don't know yet."

"Who for?"

"I don't know yet."

He looked down at his plate, trying to think of
something both inspiring and supportive. Something
that made her see that light everyone's supposed to see
at some point. She spoke before he thought of anything
meaningful.

"Dad, it'll work out."

He gave her a crooked smile and changed the subject.
If her mother were alive he would have been able to be
the bad guy. To talk some sense into her. Shelley could
have been the one to agree with her at all costs. The one
to support her blindly. Since she died, Keith could never
find the balance. He erred on the side of the blind sup-
porter.

Elle stood on the staircase, and looked down on

her father on the couch. It had always amused her how much their house resembled the house from the Cosby Show. The front door leading into the family room with a staircase against the far wall. A door into the kitchen, another staircase.

Her father was stretched out on the couch, facing the TV. From her place on the fifth stair from the top, Elle couldn't see if his eyes were closed or focused on the solitary figure on the screen. A man was running through the city, everything was black and white. He picked up a football looking directly at Keith on the couch and a message popped up under him, "Football my anti-drug."

The black and white of the screen was immediately replaced with color—a newborn in a crib, a mother with a wide smile, and an amazingly absorptive diaper. The mother held the baby by the ankles, exposing her diaper-rash-free butt, and then put on another diaper. The mother flashed a white smile and the child never wriggled or cried, the picture of perfection. Her father rolled over on the couch, stared at the ceiling briefly, and then caught Elle in the corner of his eye.

"Hey, what are you doing standing up there?"

Elle stepped down three steps, and jumped the last two.

"I wasn't sure if you were sleeping and I didn't want to wake you."

She sat in the navy blue armchair, its back to the front door, perpendicular to the couch. From that angle, Elle could see only half the TV. Keith turned it off and directed all his attention to her. He lifted his arms above his head, stretching, and yawned.

"I'm so glad to have you home, Elle."

"I'm glad to be home, dad. It's nice to get out of the dorms for awhile. Nice to not live in one, small room."

It always made Elle sad to think of her father lying

on the couch every night. Alone. She remembered coming home over an hour after her twelve o'clock curfew to find her mother and father sitting on the couch, shoulder to shoulder, talking. They hadn't been waiting up for her, they had just lost track of time.

For Keith, the couch had become the closest he could get to Shelley. They spent so many hours just sitting, just talking, just cuddling. The cemetery never did anything for him. There are no memories of them there, nothing shared there. The bedroom was too painful. As he sat on the couch, he relived their plans. He relived the moments that he had imagined would happen, he relived his life before the accident. Sometimes, when Elle was away at school, he slept on the couch with a box of tissues.

"So, dad, tell me what you've been up to."

"Well." He stretched. "Things at the office are good. No one's doing anything too interesting really."

Her father lived for small talk—from others. He answered most questions about himself with vague, direction-less answers. He worked in a small firm in Bryn Mawr, defending tax evaders, insurance frauds, and other white-collar criminals.

"How are the Sixers' doing so far? I haven't really followed them this year."

"Oh, Elle. Gotta follow the Sixers. They started off slow. 0 and 5. Iverson was out with his shoulder surgery recovery. But once they got him back the team came together the way they should. They're looking strong, Elle. Hoping for another run this year."

Elle smiled at her father. Mention sports and he can talk forever. Keith watched his daughter closely. Was the conversation boring to her? She didn't want to talk about sports. He ventured a change in subject.

"So how was the semester, Elle?"

He wasn't positive, but he felt pretty sure he had asked

her this question, or versions quite similar to it, multiple times since she had been home. She humored him.

"Well...it was good. My classes were great. Everything was relevant to what I want to do. Everything had a point."

Keith struggled to keep the question down, or at least keep it silently running through his head—what do you want to do? He stretched again and forced a smile.

"That's great Elle. How was Erin?"

"She's good, she's actually going to be in Philly tomorrow to shop with her mom. I might go into the city for lunch with them."

"Oh great. That'll be nice..."

They talked until Elle's head began to bob between consciousness and sleep. Keith, flat on the couch, watched her eyes flutter. Her naturally tan skin brushed against the upholstery of the chair as sleep overtook her.

"Elle, Elle. Elle, honey."

She didn't respond, she was sleeping deeply. She looked so mature to him. When she went to college she still had that look lying somewhere between excitement and fear. Now midway through her junior year, calmness had overtaken her. Keith saw a calm innocence, others would disagree.

There was comfort in Elle curled on the armchair, him on the couch. There was comfort in not being alone in the house. The night his wife died, he and Elle both slept in this room. Too stunned to move themselves upstairs, too exhausted to notice where they were. Elle had slept on the couch this night, he sat on the blue arm-chair, completely upright, completely awake.

One phrase came to Keith every time he thought about his wife's death. What a waste. What a waste of a death. She was the type that should have died publicly, in a heroic act—saving a crippled child from a speeding produce truck, carrying an elderly nun out of a burning convent. Shelley was the type of person who found herself in situations so outrageous and so random that they became somehow meaningful. Her death should have accomplished something.

It was early fall, Elle had just gone off the college. Keith was at work and Shelley planned her day around cleaning the windows. She had refused to let Keith put new windows into the house. These are more authentic. They're meant to be in this house. Shelley always said things like that. On a warm September day, she got the Windex, the paper towels, and climbed the ledge carefully, in order to reach the top corners. The windows were so old, made from heavy, thick wood. She started in Elle's room. Then the bathroom. Her bedroom last. The side window and left-most front window were sparkling when they found her. She was cleaning her last window.

No one could tell Keith exactly what happened. There were no witnesses. But Keith saw the accident very clearly in his sleep.

Shelley finished the left-most front window and moved directly to the right-most front window. She could see the whole neighborhood as she leaned forward out the open window. With her hands on the windowpane, arms straight, she stuck her head into the fresh air. She smelled leaves burning and immediately thought of bagpipes. The only time Shelley had heard live bagpipes was at her great uncle's burial. Next to the cemetery, a young woman stood beside a pile of burning leaves. The scent drifted over the funeral party, hanging over the coffin before drifting past the red and yellow leaves still on the trees, awaiting the same fate. It was a childhood memory, surfacing over Kettle One and a soft couch, that Shelley relived late one night, the side of her face pressed snugly into Keith's sweater.

Her shoulder blades were an inch below the open window when some spring or latch snapped and the heavy wood crashed down. She heard the click, and instinctively braced her shoulders for impact. She guided the window down, eased herself inside, and disappeared inside the house. Minutes later she was balancing backwards out the same window, which was now held open by a greased cookie sheet.

Her butt and right hand rested against the window-pane and her left hand wiped back and forth in a consistent motion. She hummed. Shelley didn't rush, the weather was too nice, the air too warm, life too perfect. She spent over ten minutes sitting backwards in that window-pane, she had no where to go.

The neighborhood was covered in a mid-morning quiet. The kids were at school, the husbands and working wives were at work, the stay-at-home moms were food shopping. So the cutting ring of the phone was even more startling than usual. Maybe that's why she jumped at the first ring, nearly falling backwards out the window. The second ring must have been just as disruptive to the perfect afternoon silence. It rushed her. She slid her butt into the house, turned onto her stomach, and swung her elbows back in one smooth motion. Her left elbow caught the cookie sheet, knocking it onto the hardwood floor. It clattered, though Shelley probably never heard it.

As the rest of her torso followed the swinging motion of her arms and lower body, the window, uninhibited by the cookie sheet, fell smoothly, with violent force. Had her head, her soft dark hair, slid through the window just before it clamped shut, it would have been a beautiful thing: the sweeping movement of her body racing against the raging power of gravity, and winning. But the thick wood met her neck. There was an unnatural crunch, there was a clatter of a cookie sheet, there was silence.

In some dreams, his wife dies instantly as the heavy wood clamps shut. Her last sight a green blur of grass beneath her as she rushes into the house backwards. The snap of her neck cuts off her breath—her life—the moment the unnatural crack interrupts the beautiful fall mid-morning quiet. Her should length hair hangs out the window, moving with the changing wind.

In the other version, the force of the falling window paralyzes Shelley. She's alive as the heavy wood cuts into her neck, blackness slowly filling her eyes. Minutes, hours. She can't feel anything below where the wood rests on her neck. She can't feel anything but fear. Her breath shortens as air struggles through her trachea, she sees her husband, her daughter, thick wood, brick, darkness. She smells burning leaves, she hears bagpipes.

Keith woke up violently that night to find Elle still asleep on the armchair. He is sweating, breathing heavily, and shaking. He was dreaming about Shelley—no, about her death. He knew he should wake Elle, have her go sleep in her own bed. But that would mean that he has to go sleep is his own bed, with the moonlight spilling in that window.

He sat upright on the couch, and then leaned back, exhaling. She had rushed because the phone was ringing. When he came home form work, the ambulance was already there. A neighbor saw her head, her delicate hair hanging unnaturally from beneath the heavy window. She was dead before anyone arrived. She died alone.

The phone call. After the medical personnel, police, and investigators left, Keith walked around house with his eyes wide, like he was looking for her. The message light on the answering machine blinked, he hit play. It was a courtesy call. A man with a lisp asking for money for orphaned children in the tri-state area. Even then, Keith recognized the irony. She died trying to get to a phone to talk to a man with a lisp who would have asked for money. She would have said yes, been generous, and helped a parent-less kid. That wasn't heroic enough. She deserved more than that. He threw the answering machine to the ground and beat it with the heel of his foot until the blinking stopped.

When she woke in the morning, Elle was stiff from sleeping in a ball on the armchair. Her father had left for work already. She found a note on the polished coffee table—Sorry, I fell asleep down here too. Hope you're not to sore. By the time Erin called at twelve-thirty, Elle was finally starting to loosen the kink in her neck.

"Hey! Sorry, we just got finished with shopping."

"Oh, that's okay."

"Listen, why don't we meet you somewhere near your house? My mom knows where the King Street Grill is. Is that close to you?"

"Yeah, very close. What time should I be there?"

Elle was there before Erin and her mom. She sat outside on the steps, waiting in the unusually warm December afternoon. They pulled up in a white Blazer. Erin hopped out and the car pulled away.

"Hey Er! Isn't your mom coming?"

"Yeah, she'll be here—she saw some shop she wanted to go into. She told me what she was in the mood to eat, so it's not a big deal."

They followed the hostess to a corner table for three. Elle and Erin sat next to each other, both facing the restaurant. Elle rested her feet on the empty chair saved for

Mrs. Creeto. There was an excited look in Erin's eyes.

"Elle, so how are you going to get stuff?"

"What?"

"It's four and a half weeks. Where else can you get stuff besides me? Now, what I'm offering you isn't white or anything—but hell, Elle, it's something."

"I'm not going to smoke in my house, Er. I'm sure I'll be able to at parties, but I don't need my own winter break stash. Seriously."

Disappointment spread over Erin's face, though Elle was to busy playing with a sugar pack to notice. Without looking at Erin, Elle continued.

"Besides, I don't have any money."

"Elle, come on. It never has to be about money."

"I'm not going to use it, Er." There was some finality in her voice. "I'm going to the bathroom, if the waitress comes, order me a grilled cheese and a glass of milk."

"Milk?"

Elle walked away and Erin watched her friend disappear into the bathroom. A thoughtful look spread across her face. She swung her purse—a large, camel-colored leather bag—onto her lap. She unzipped the built-in change purse along the side of her bag, then slipped her hand into a hole ripped into the lining. Erin ran her fingers along the inside of the camel leather, until she felt a smooth plastic against her skin. Pretending to be totally engrossed in a cosmetics mirror she had placed on the table, Erin pulled the plastic bag out of the change purse.

Erin watched the door, neither her mother nor Elle were in sight. She pulled Elle's jacket off the back of her chair, slipped the plastic bag into the pocket, and zipped it closed. She smile thinking—she'll thank me later. With her covert mission accomplished, Erin sat at the table waiting for Elle to take her seat. Once Elle was sitting, Erin would wait until her mother entered the restaurant, saw the table, and began her approach, before whispering to Elle--check your pockets. Then she'd wink and Elle would know the gift was safely there. With Erin's mother walking towards them, there was no way Elle could refuse the pot or attempt a return.

In the bathroom, Elle stood in front of the toilet, leaning against the stall door, with no intention of moving. What was Erin trying to do? For four weeks Elle just wanted to be what her father thought she was. Just for four weeks. When her mother was alive, Elle never felt guilty about smoking. It was her father—alone, singular. Looking at Elle like she was the only thing pure in his world—that made the guilt come. She waited in the stall until she was sure Erin's mom was at the table. She wanted to make fake conversation, talk to adults, act like she was still a child. The cold metal of the stall began to sting Ell's forehead.

Erin saw the Blazer pull into the parking lot, Elle still had not come out of the bathroom. She watched her mother enter the restaurant, spot her in the corner, and begin to walk towards the table. A loud slam startled Mrs. Creeto as she passed the bathrooms. Elle stepped into view and the two exchanged glances and laughs. They sat down with Erin at the same time.

"I ordered for both of you."

"Thanks Erin."

Elle and Erin's mom responded at the same time, in the same tone. The restaurant was a small place. The wall facing the street was lined with windows and tables, all of which were empty. Though Elle, Erin and Mrs. Creeto occupied one of only three other occupied tables in the restaurant, their table was stuck away from light, in the corner, near the swinging kitchen doors. Their waiter was a short, stocky teenager. It was obvious that he dreaded serving tables of the opposite sex. When he arrived with water, he nervously scratched at the dry skin and acne framing his face. They hadn't seen him since. The conversation was strong for the first ten minutes.

"Elle, tell me, how was your semester?"

"It was a lot of fun, Mrs. Creeto. Every class was interesting and relevant."

Erin rolled her eyes, though only Elle noticed it. It was amusing to Erin that Elle could sound so studious, so serious. Erin's look made Elle uncomfortable, a feeling interrupted by the arrival of their lunches.

The waiter stuttered and fumbled as he presented the food.

"The Grilled Cheese…the Chicken Caesar Salad…the Mandarin Chicken Salad. Can I get you girls something else?"

Elle looked at the lunch sitting in front of her, instantly jealous of the towering piles of lettuce surrounding her buttered and fried bread. She wished Erin hadn't been so annoying and she had been able to actually look over the menu.

"I'll take a cranberry juice, please."

"Oh, Elle, I love cranberry juice." She smiled dutifully at Mrs. Creeto. Silence covered the table as they ate. From her seat Erin watched the waiter emerge form the swinging doors with the tall glass of cranberry juice balanced on his tray. She saw his left foot catch the leg of an extra chair positioned between the kitchen and their table of three. Though she made a forced, guttural noise, there was nothing she could do to stop the chain of events. Foot catches, waiter falls, cranberry juice slides off tray towards the khaki jacket hanging loosely on the back of Elle's chair, a crash.

When they had finished eating, Elle examined her khaki jacket. It was fitted in the back, where the red burst now was. The pockets, which she rarely used, were zippered shut. The collar was lined with gray cotton. She draped her favorite jacket over her arm as they exited the restaurant. A manager chased after her, offering one more apology and giving her a gift certificate. The incident didn't upset Elle; she'd be able to get the stain out—or at least most of it. And she got a free lunch.

Elle refused the offer from Mrs. Creeto, and insisted on walking home on such a warm winter day. Standing next to the pavement, she waved and watched as Erin and her mother turned right and the white Blazer disappeared into traffic. As Elle turned left and stepped onto the sidewalk, she could see the clock tower, she could see the bridge, the train tracks, and what used to be her mother's favorite bar—Hair of the Dog. But she had lost sight of the white Blazer, and there was no possible way she could see Erin stiffen as she thought about the khaki jacket, the red stain, the zippered pockets, and the hidden gift.

Once home, Elle sat on the couch, flickering though the channels. Soap operas and talk shows annoyed her. Info-mercials bored her. MTV targeted pre-teens. She couldn't stand the Dating Story. Standing, with the remote in hand, she ambled towards the stairs, still flipping channels, hoping to find something to watch at the last minute. At the fifth stair to the top, she stopped, turned the TV off, placed the remote on the staircase and disappeared upstairs.

When her father came home from work at 5:45 he almost forgot she was home. He was so used to coming home to emptiness. The house was quiet, but Keith checked the entire first floor before climbing the stairs to Elle's room. He picked up remote up, leaned over the railing, and tossed it gently on the couch. It landed with a soft thud on the cushions, bounced and hit the floor with a clatter.

The door to Elle's room was slightly open, it creaked

as Keith gently pushed into the room. Leaning against the doorframe, he could see his daughter curled on the bed. An open book rested on her right arm, her left hand covered by the paperback spine. Her shoes were upside down, one half hidden by the bedskirt. She looked so peaceful and calm. Pushing himself off the doorframe, he turned, and walked away. Just before he reached the stairs, he realized he left her door wide open.

Keith turned back, leaned into the room, grabbed the knob, and pulled the door towards him. With his neck and head peeking between the door and the doorframe, he scanned his daughter's room. The motion drew his eyes to her desk, where her khaki jacket hung on the back of her chair. The red stain faded into the material, leaving a pastel-like circle in the center. Without a word, without a touch, Keith walked past his daughter, smiled, draped her jacket over his arm, and disappeared behind a closing door. He didn't rush—the weather was too nice, the air too warm, life nearly perfect.

Keith felt his way down the wooden steps to the laundry room. He was used to taking each step carefully, slowly, burdened by a cumbersome plastic laundry basket. With only the jacket in his arms, it was easy for him to slip down the dark stairs. Yet, somehow he misjudged the second to the last step, and tripped forward into the wall. He laughed at himself, and pulled himself upright. The fall made a soft thud, if anything, not nearly loud enough to wake Elle.

But at the same moment, or nearly, Elle rolled over and looked at her clock. Her father would be home soon. On her back, surrounded by the soft down comforter, she stared at the ceiling waiting to hear him come in. He fumbled through the darkness two floors below Elle, her stained jacket in his right hand, his left fingers grasping the thin string, pulling.

apprentice
house

Apprentice House is the future of publishing...today. Using state-of-the-art technology and an experiential learning model of education, it publishes books in untraditional ways while teaching tomorrow's future editors and publishers.

Staffed by students, this non-profit activity of the Department of Communication at Loyola College in Maryland is part of an advanced elective course and overseen by the press's Director. When class is not in session, work on book projects is carried forward by a co-curricular organization, The Apprentice House Book Publishing Club, of which the press's Director also serves as Faculty Advisor.

Contributions are welcomed to sustain the press's work and are tax deductible to the fullest extent allowed by the IRS. For more information, see www.apprenticehouse.com.

Student Editors (2005-06)

Cook Alciati '06
Michael Barry '05
Michelle Betton '05
Jeff Bradley '05
Kristen Cesiro '07
Katie Dailey '06
Christine DeSanctis '05
Elizabeth Didora '05
Michael Hilt '05

Lauren Galvin '05
Marion Goodworth '05
Morgan Hillenbrand '05
Michael Hilt '05
Patricia McNamara '06
Lindsay Miller '05
Kathleen Nagle '05
Kerri Reilly '05
Erik Schmitz '07